TINCUP

CW01496910

ALSO BY B.N. RUNDELL

Rindin' Lonesome

Star Dancer

The Christmas Bear

Buckskin Chronicles

McCain Chronicles

Plainsman Western Series

Rocky Mountain Saint Series

Stonecroft Saga

The Quest Chronicles

TINCUP

A QUEST CHRONICLES NOVEL
BOOK 2

B.N. RUNDELL

WOLFPACK
PUBLISHING
— EST 2013 —

TinCup
Paperback Edition
Copyright © 2024 B.N. Rundell

Wolfpack Publishing
1707 E. Diana Street
Tampa, FL 33610

wolfpackpublishing.com

Paperback ISBN 978-1-63977-538-5
eBook ISBN 978-1-63977-537-8
LCCN 2024941359

To the unnamed, the unknown, and the unheard.

TINCUP

1

NORTH

THEY REINED UP AT THE CREST OF PONCHA PASS AND TURNED back to look at the north end of the San Luis Valley, a valley with untold history of Mexican sheepherders bringing their herds north into the fertile valley for the summer to fatten and breed, a valley that had been the home of several different bands of the Ute people and even some Comanche, Jicarilla Apache and others. This was where Cordell Beckett had brought the former captive of the Kiowa, Yellow Singing Bird, home to her people, the Caputa Ute. They were told her family had crossed over and the only one that remained was a sister, Night Wind, but when her friend, Cord, left, Bird chose to follow and now rode beside him.

It was in this valley, this same day, that Cord had been rudely introduced to the bruin of the black timber, a silvertip grizzly boar that gave Cord an invitation to leave his land and Cord willingly obliged. Now the two, friends but not lovers, sat side by side, taking in the majesty of the wide valley that separated the distant

San Juan Mountains on the west, and the long line of
Sangre de Cristo mountains on the east. This was the
northernmost point and the beginning of the Sangre de
Cristo range, with a dark green humped foothill that
ushered the taller mountains to the south. Cord
marveled at the uniformed Sangres like parading
sentinels that seemed to march in lockstep to the south
bedecked in dark blue, almost black tunics that flared
out below broad shoulders in grey jackets with white
adornments, sharp tipped helmets in matching grey
granite, all silently but majestically marching single file
to the south and out of sight.

In was coming on late afternoon as they turned to
ride through the white-barked aspen that stood
proudly with heart-shaped leaves fluttering in the mild
breeze that came from the higher mountains and
dropped through the narrow but lonely valleys. It was a
quiet afternoon, a clear blue sky arching overhead, and
warm sunshine filtering through the aspen leaves to
warm the shoulders of the two travelers. Cord was
pleased that Bird choose to come with him, but he was
also troubled at what lay ahead. He was determined to
find the outlaws that had gone by the moniker of Bushwhackers or Red Legs when they rode in gangs during
the war, but their evil ways continued even after the
war had ended, and it was then they hit the home of
Cordell Beckett and his family. Although a teen at the
time and gone into the woods for some time alone with
his new books, the assault began with gunfire that
drew Cord from his getaway and into the trees near his
home, but his home was already ablaze, his father's
body sprawled on the steps, and his mother, brother,

and sister trapped inside. The brigands looted the home and barn, left everything ablaze, and ran off, leaving Cord to pick up the pieces of what remained of his life.

He spent the next few years growing up and arming and equipping himself with weapons, skills, and information to begin his search for the outlaws and his vengeance. But the teachings of his preacher father continually haunted his spirit and consciousness with reminders of scriptures and teachings of life principles of forgiveness and kindness, but he did his best to silence those memories and rekindle his burning desire for justice and vengeance.

His search brought him west from Missouri, following the Santa Fe Trail and scouting and hunting for a freighter outfit. It was on that journey that he found three of the men, one reformed his ways and was not a part of the raid on Cord's farm, another had left the gang and was nothing but a drunk they left behind, and the third was killed when Cord helped a stage that was being robbed by some masked bandits. But there were still many left on the list he compiled when talking to Bill Tough, the reformed outlaw, and Duncan Pitts, the man who had become the drunk. Cord did not seek vengeance on those men, choosing to leave the reformed outlaw to his own memories, and the drunk to his self-destructive ways.

Now he was headed north to gold country and a diggings called California Gulch, where the outlaws were rumored to be working. He knew they would be after easy money, preferring to kill and rob rather than do an honest day's work, and in the gold fields, there was seldom any lawmen and little if any chance of retribution for their wicked ways. And Cord was still struggling with three words that haunted his sleep, vengeance, justice, and forgiveness. He was not a lawman, but he had been taught the necessity of good men standing for what is right and when they fail to stand for justice and right, evil will prevail, and good men will pay the price of their own negligence. That was the result of sitting through his father's many sermons in the little country church in the little community of Harrisonville, Missouri, as well as the many personal lessons at and sometimes on his father's knee.

Cord was a tall man, with a flat-brimmed dark felt hat worn low over his dark brows and full face of whiskers, always wearing a long tan duster, canvas britches, and linen shirt, he was a handsome man, whenever he chose to show his face, and usually preferred silence over talking. He rode a line-back dun, grulla stallion, and led the pack mule loaded with the extra gear. He had a Henry .44 in the scabbard under his right leg, a Sharps .50 in the scabbard under his left leg, a Remington New model Army .44 pistol in a holster on his left hip, butt forward, a Bowie knife in a sheath between his shoulder blades and easily reached behind his neck, and a coach gun shotgun in the pack on the mule. Trotting alongside his long-legged grulla was a scruffy looking but faithful hound dog that answered to the name of Blue. Beside Cord rode Yellow Singing Bird, who went by the name Bird, and wore beaded and fringed buckskin tunic over beaded and fringed leggings and matching moccasins. She sat astride a flashy gelding, traded from her sister's man who wanted her white mare for breeding and made her a good trade for the appaloosa gelding he had acquired in a trade from the Nez Percé, well known for their fine horses. Bird also carried a Henry .44 in a scabbard, but preferred her bow and arrow for most hunting in close-in work. She had a razor-sharp skinning Green River knife and could wield it as well as throw it and had the skill, dexterity, and agility to be quite formidable in a fight, which she had proven.

As they neared the edge of the aspen grove, Cord frowned and reined up. He stood in his stirrups and bent side to side to look through the thicket of white trunked aspen. He lifted his eyes high, saw circling turkey buzzards and turned to look back at Bird, motioning her to step down and hold the animals. Cord also swung down, rifle in hand and with a quick check of his pistol, he dropped into a crouch and began picking his way through the trees. The matted leaves still held the moisture from the night and the rain from a couple days past, and his moccasined feet moved soundlessly through the thicket. He dropped to one knee at the edge of the trees, frowned and slowly stood, shaded his eyes from the lowering sun, and looked all about for any sign of trouble. Satisfied, he motioned Bird forward and pointed below where the trail crossed Poncha Creek at the bottom of the long ravine that carried the water to the valley below. Just beyond the crossing, the remains of a wagon smoldered, and carrion eaters were gathering to feed on the dead carcasses of two horses, still in harness where they lay.

Cord recognized the wagon and horses as a wagon of movers they helped the day before when they met at the hot springs. Three women and two wounded men were the last of a wagon train that had been attacked by some Jicarilla Apache in the southern part of San Luis Valley. Cord and Bird had helped them bind up the wounds of the men, and Cord gave them directions to cross the pass and follow the road northeast to the bottom and the new settlement of Poncha Springs. He thought they would be safe, but he warned them of the possibility of the remains of a Comanche war party that might come up the same trail.

He shook his head as they walked closer and saw the mutilated remains of the women, the men had probably died in the wagon where they lay helpless and wounded. He sighed heavily as he glanced to Bird whose eyes were squinted and nostrils flaring as she thought of the hated Comanche. It had been the Comanche who had captured her as a child, kept her in their village for a couple years, then traded her to the Kiowa, and it was there she was found by Cord. They had fought some of the Comanche, killed four, and left the valley of the Arkansas to come to her people in the San Luis Valley, but now they would travel through the valley to go to California Gulch, further to the north and near the headwaters of the Arkansas River.

As Cord neared the wagons, he looked at Bird, "We need to bury them." He pointed with his chin at the bluff that fell from the higher foothills, "There. I'll dig it out a bit, and we can cave the bank over 'em. Don't know their full names, ain't nuthin' left of their stuff, so won't bother with a marker. You look things over, if you find anything, lay it aside, I'll start digging."

He lifted the neckerchief over his nose and mouth, the terrible stench of burning flesh was disgusting, but decency demanded they be buried.

Dusk was settling over the mountains, filling the valleys and ravines with darker shadows, and softening the looks of the land, silence seemed to accompany the darker shades, and Cord and Bird rode into the little settlement of Poncha Springs, where they had been just three days back, but now it lay silent in the muted light.

2

CHALK CREEK

"No, they musta passed through the trees after dark. We din't see any Comanche or any others!" declared John Burnett as he stood in the door of his log trading post. Burnett was the Indian Agent for the area and the Ute people, and had also been the man Cord and Bird had visited with earlier when the Comanche and Cheyenne were coming into the valley, intent on raids and stealing horses, but ended up in a fight between them. Many of the settlers feared an attack on their homes or the village, but after their fight, both war parties chose to return to the villages.

"Well, they went through here, come on a wagon of settlers that were the last of a wagon train that had been attacked by the Jicarilla, we helped 'em a mite, but after the wagon came down into the valley, crossed the creek, they musta run into the Comanche and the war party killed 'em all, burnt the wagon and more," explained Cord. "We're glad they didn't hit you folks, we were a mite concerned about that."

Burnett looked from Cord to Bird, "Thought you were lookin' for your people. Couldn't you find them?"

Bird glanced to Cord with a smile, "We found them, but the only family that remains is a sister and her man. I chose to stay with Cord," she smiled as she slipped her hand through the crook of his elbow as they stood before the agent.

Cord glanced to the morning sky that showed promise of a clear day and looked to Burnett, "We'll be headin' out. Got a ways to go."

"Still lookin' for them Red Legs?"

"Ummhmm, any news?"

"None."

"Then we'll be goin'," added Cord, stepping back to swing aboard Kwitcher, his big grulla stallion.

Bird swung up on her appaloosa, smiled at Cord and they rode from the little village. Their route took them along the flanks of the Sawatch Mountains, always moving north, bound for California Gulch, the 'hot spot' of gold country. But they had heard before about Chalk Creek and that there were some early diggings up that gulch and the bushwhackers were said to be seen up there. The search for the outlaws had been the driving purpose of Cord's life for the last three, going on four, years and even though he had been having some doubts about the right of it, he was not ready to let go and forgive them like the preacher back to Fort Lyon had said he should and what his father had often preached.

He remembered the preacher with the wagons back at Fort Lyon had said, "Ephesians 4:32 says...*forgiving one another, even as God for Christ's sake hath forgiven you.*"

Cord shook his head at the thought of forgiving the outlaws for murdering his family and burning his home, but he knew the scriptures spoke often about forgiveness, yet he held to Luke 17:3 *Take heed to yourselves: If thy brother trespass against thee, rebuke him; and if he repent, forgive him.* Cord let a slow grin split his face as he rode in silent thought, thinking more about *rebuke him,* which meant to confront and correct them, and he resolved his thoughts with his focus on the rebuke coming before repentance and forgiveness. He breathed deep, looking around and focusing on the land about them.

The Sawatch Mountains, looking bigger than the Sangre de Cristo mountains, but still the granite-tipped peaks that stretched high above timberline and with black or dark-blue skirts of timber the covered the lower reaches, marched to the north, their broad shoulders spreading wide, but showing clefts that marked the different peaks and ofttimes passages over the range. The crevices between peaks still held glaciers and snowdrifts, accenting the ruggedness of the massive mountains. Cord slowed, stood in his stirrups and took a deep breath of the cool mountain air, grinning as he sat back, looking to Bird. "Love it! This is my kinda country!"

Bird smiled, nudged her appaloosa closer and pointed, "Those are the Chalk Cliffs, where the creek gets its name." She pointed to what looked like a big white scab on the lower flank of the broad shoulder of another towering mountain.

"Are they chalk? They don't look white, more of a pale grey," remarked Cord, frowning as he shaded his eyes to look at the rare sight of rocky hips on the big mountain.

"I do not know, chalk. It is rock, not hard, but the hot water comes from the cracks and carves the cliffs. It makes pools at the bottom," she pointed to the thin wisps of steam rising near the base of the cliffs. "The man at the trading post said this is where the creek is called Chalk Creek."

Cord sighed, slowly shaking his head, "Then let's go," he resolved. Although the mountain and its rocky hips were still a couple miles away, the morning was passing and with fresh water there, it would be a good place for their nooning. And such it proved to be, as they crested the ridge of the long alluvial plain that fell from the mountains on the west edge of the Arkansas River valley, the long ridge that was thick with juniper, piñon, and scrub oak, stood above the long valley that had been carved eons ago by the meandering Chalk Creek. While the long alluvial plain that fell from the forested skirts of the Sawatch Mountains, it extended itself to the east toward the river and appeared like long tentacles or fingers reaching for the fertile flats. But Cord's attention was focused on the remarkable cliff faces that had been carved as they stood boldly overlooking the long valley showing their own low shoulders that were dimpled with the same trees and brush found on the slope they now were winding their way through to make it to the chuckling creek below.

They edged up to the creek, looking about at the willows, chokecherry bushes, some kinnikinnick, and the low-growing berry crawlers. As they slid to the ground, Cord breathed deep of the cool mountain air, taking in the scents of the bushes about him, but also the pungent scent of piñon and juniper. The sweat of the horses lifted from beside him, and when Blue rolled in the water, there was no mistaking the smell of wet dog, and Cord chuckled at the antics of his companion hound and long-legged grulla stallion that pushed his way into the water as well, prompting Bird's appaloosa gelding to follow. The horses were still getting acquainted and kept their distance when the mule pushed between them, for the big mule brokered no argument from either one, as he bared his teeth and laid his long ears back to let his intentions be known.

Bird tossed the reins of her appy to Cord, "I'll get some wood, we'll have some coffee and maybe more," and turned away to push her way through the willows. Cord watched her walk away, still wondering about her resolve to stay with him, but even with all the questions, he was glad to have her company. He stepped back from water's edge, pushed his hat back on his head, and lifted his eyes to the rocky cliffs that climbed the steep shoulders of the mountain across the way. He frowned when he saw movement and some dusty brown shapes that seemed to be cavorting about on the steep rocky face of the mountain. He looked around for Bird, saw a thin wisp of smoke rising on the far side of the willows and started her direction. She was kneeling near the fire, pushing the coffee pot closer and looked up as Cord approached. He tethered the animals to a nearby juniper and turned, pointed to the cliffs, "You see that over there? Looks like a bunch o' them bighorn sheep playin' tag on the mountain!"

They watched as the herd, mostly ewes and lambs, with a few young rams, came off the rocky escarpments and began to graze on the grass that lay in the shadows of the cliffs. As they watched, two of the young rams began to joust with one another, standing off, staring at one another, slowly rising to their hind feet, heads cocked to the side, then dropping to all fours and charging with heads down to clash together, their horns colliding and sounding like a gunshot as the crack echoed across the valley and back again. Cord chuckled, looked to Bird who was watching the rams as much as she was watching Cord and she smiled, "They are preparing for the time in the late summer, early fall, when the breeding happens. The winner takes all!" she declared with a slight giggle and a coy smile to Cord.

After their brief respite, they pushed on into the mountains. The valley of the Chalk Creek split the massive mountain range but by no deed of man, the creek came from the higher mountains and had followed the path lined out by the Creator as he pushed the mountains aside for the little stream. The trail hugged the face on the south side of the creek, and had probably been nothing more than a game trail, but it showed signs of recent travel and was primary trail into the mountains. The broad shoulders of the mountains occasionally pushed the creek one way or the other, forcing the waterway to carve its own way through the rocky abutments, often cascading down steep rockfaces making whitewater splash about, crashing its way below.

At one point when the trail pushed around a point of rock that lay in the shadow of a steep rock face that marked the bare shoulders of a north side mountain, and the trail crossed a low saddle, Cord reined up and stood in his stirrups to gaze at the long valley before him. Mountains on either side stood as sentries, looking down on the miniscule visitors to the quiet valley between the columns of mountains. Cord looked at Bird, shook his head and showed a wide grin, "Sure wish my pa coulda seen this! Mountains stacked on mountains and stretching as far as the eye can see!" He pointed before them, "That little valley looks like a green snake slithering between the buttes!"

Bird smiled and nodded, "Do you believe we will find those you follow?"

"Maybe, but I doubt it. I reckon they've prob'ly gone somewhere else by now. But all we can do it follow. If we don't find out somethin' by the time we get to the end of this valley, we'll try somethin' else," he shrugged and nudged Kwitcher on, keeping to the trail that pointed to the trees on the south side of the valley.

It was late afternoon, and the sun was dropping into the notch between the mountains, giving the shadows of the valleys boldness to make themselves known. As the black timber embraced the coming darkness, the mountain peaks seemed to grab the last of the light and painted themselves in golden hues, shading to pinks and oranges. As they looked about, they came to a confluence of creeks that formed the bigger Chalk Creek, the smaller creeks coming from separate valleys, one that pointed due west, the other splitting the peaks on the south, with a stretch of granite-tipped peaks dividing the two creeks. The trail also split with a branch of trail following each fork of the stream.

Cord looked about and as he shaded his eyes from the lowering sun, Bird stepped down and went to the fork of the trail, dropped to one knee and examined some tracks. She looked up the trail to the left that came from the south, and then to her right across the creek. With another look at the tracks, she said, "One man, walking, other tracks are of a colt or small horse...?" She frowned as she glanced to the tracks again. Standing and shading her eyes, she pointed to the distant trees across the creek, "There!"

3

FOREST CITY

BELOW THEM ON THE FAR SIDE OF THE CREEK, WHERE BIRD was pointing, Cord saw a patch of dingy white showing through the trees and thought he recognized a wall tent with logs as a frame of lower walls. The back end was tucked under the wide-spreading branches of a big spruce and the rickety tin chimney loosed a thin wisp of smoke that climbed into the branches to be swallowed before reaching the treetops. Standing in front of the tent, two smaller trees shielded it from view, but the off-color gave it away.

Cord nodded, "Looks like there's somebody got 'em a tent over yonder, let's go see what he can tell us."

Bird swung back aboard her appy and followed Cord as he led the pack mule and started across the creek. It was up a slight rise to a flat shoulder covered with juniper and scattered spruce and an occasional ponderosa, and nothing was amiss, but a dim trail split the trees, as pointed out by Bird, and Cord nudged his mount into the trees.

They pulled up at the edge of a slight clearing,

seeing the wall tent sheltered in the thicker stand of pines, and Cord called out, "Hello the camp! We're friendly and wanna talk!"

Nothing moved or stirred, no answer came from the tent, but Blue took a tentative step forward, one paw lifted and a low growl coming from deep in his chest, but Blue was looking to the side of the tent in the darker shadows. A voice answered Blue's growl with a low growl of its own, "I've got a scattergun leveled at yore belly, buster. If you wanna live past sunset, it might be best for you to turn around and skedaddle!"

At the first sound of a voice, Cord slowly dropped his hand to the butt of his pistol inside his loose duster and nodded as he answered, "Now hold on, mister. We just want some information, and we'll get outta yore hair!"

"Then git that hand outta yore coat and lift 'em both high. You too woman!"

Cord nodded to Bird and slowly lifted his hands high. The voice called out again, "Keep 'em covered John!" and the branches parted and a scruffy, bearded old sourdough came from the trees, coach gun shotgun cradled in his arms. He snarled as he looked at his two visitors, stepped a little closer and looked at Cord, glanced to Bird, "Alright, what'chu want?"

Cord asked, "Can we put our hands down?"

"Go 'head on, but don't try for that pistol nor that pigsticker b'hind yore neck. You won't live long 'nuff to fall off'n yore horse!"

"Alright, alright, easy now, we mean you no harm," answered Cord, and took a deep breath as he began to explain about the Red Legs. As he finished, he added, "Couple fellas down to Poncha and Cleora said they heard those men mighta come up this way, so, we're lookin'."

"Ummhmm," he paused, glared at Cord, "Them Red Legs, what'chu gonna do with 'em if'n you find 'em?"

Cord dropped his eyes, chuckled a little, "If I have my way, I'd hang 'em by their heels an' skin 'em alive, then build a fire under their leftovers and watch 'em burn!"

"Dang! You got'chu a powerful lot o' hate goin'on there!"

"Wouldn'tchu? If they done to your family like they done to mine?" grumbled Cord.

"Din'tchu say your pappy was a preacher?"

"Ummhmm, so?"

The gruffy prospector dropped his eyes, looked up again and answered, "Don't the Good Book say *Vengeance is mine, I will repay, saith the Lord.?*"

Cord slowly shook his head, feeling the sting of God's Word and looked at the old sourdough, "But it also says, *It is more blessed to give than to receive,* and I've been on the receivin' end and it's about time I did a little of my own givin'!" he growled.

The old sourdough frowned at Cord, glanced to Bird and said, "Step on down, might have some coffee on the cookfire..." suggested the old man. He started to turn, paused, added, "Muh name is Abner Wright, muh partner in the trees yonder is John Royal. What's yore handle?"

Cord chuckled as he stepped to the ground, "I'm Cordell Beckett, Cord to most folks. And this," nodding to Bird, "is Yellow Singing Bird, of the Caputa Ute people. Bird to most folks."

"Right pleased to meet'chu ma'am," nodded Abner,

glancing from her to Cord and back, "Can't say much for your pickin's in a partner, but you'll do!" He chuckled and toddled around the tent to a cookfire that smoldered behind the wall tent in the bigger part of the clearing. A corral stretched from the tent into and around some of the trees and held three long-haired burrows with curious eyes and droopy faces, standing side by side at the rails to examine the newcomers.

Abner motioned to a long grey log on the back side of the fire, and Cord followed Bird to have a seat on the log and they accepted the offered cups of coffee.

"So, to answer yore question," began Abner as John Royal came from the trees. They looked enough alike to be brothers, both with full beards that showed ample amounts of grey, long hair that covered their ears, and bright eyes that never seemed to miss anything that moved. With canvas britches held up by galluses that stretched over faded red longjohns, hobnail boots, and floppy hats, they too sat down with full steaming cups in hand.

Abner continued, "We saw a bunch like that whut came through hyar, but that was some time back. They was five or six," he paused, looked to John for confirmation and John mumbled, "more like seven."

Abner continued, "Alright, seven or so, come through hyar, but we stayed outta sight an' they never saw us, leastwise we don't think they did, an' they kept goin'. Went up the North Fork, it's a purty good trail o'er the top an' there's a lake on the other side."

"Are there any diggin's over there?" asked Cord, frowning. "The bunch I know aren't ones to do the work themselves, they're more the type to steal what others have done."

"Yeah, they's some diggin's yonder. Some fellas came through hyar a few years back, they was headed to Californy, but then they come back. One of 'em came thisaway, wantin' to go down for some supplies. He stopped, we jawed a little, an' he stopped agin' on the way back. We had him pick us up some coffee, we'd run out and was usin' roasted chicory, ain't the same," he grumbled. "Anyway," he looked to his partner, "John, what was that feller's name?"

"Fred, Fred Lotts. An' his partners was brothers, Ben an' Charlie Gray."

"That's right! It was Fred what stopped by," chuckled Abner, glancing to his partner, and continued, "Fred said the first time they came through, they stopped o'er yonder below the lake, and saw some sparkles in the water when they stopped to drink, an' you know how most men carry a tin cup hangin' on their belt, wal, they took their cups and used 'em to pan some gravel! Got 'em some color too, they done! But t'weren't 'nuff to stop, what with Californy callin', so they went on west. But that was a bust, so they come back. Built 'em a couple cabins, started callin' the place TinCup!" hehehehe, "Don' that beat all? TinCup!" Abner shook his head at the thought.

Cord looked at the old sourdough, "What'chu callin' this place?"

Abner sobered, glanced to his partner, back to Cord, "Aw, we just call it Forest City, what with all the trees. But if'n any settlers come, they'll cut down the entire forest, so we won't call it that. 'Course, we'll prob'ly be dead by then!" grumbled Abner, dropping his eyes to the fire.

"You fellas must have tried your luck everywhere round abouts, right?"

Abner frowned, reached for his coach gun that lay beside him, "Why you askin' that?"

"Whoa, din't mean nuthin'! Don't matter to us! I hadn't seen any prospect holes and we were just wonderin' if there were any others up these canyons and such that mighta seen them fellas."

"Ain't nobody else. Oh, there's been a few come through, try a few pans an' when they don't get color, they keep on goin'. We only get 'nuff to keep us in coffee an' beans. But mebbe someday!" cackled Abner, his belly bouncing on his sagging belt as he reached for the coffee pot for a refill.

Cord looked from Abner to John and then to Bird, "Well, let's be goin', Bird. We need to find us a camp, get some supper goin'."

Bird nodded, handed her cup to Abner as did Cord and they both stood to leave. Cord looked at the men, "We thank you for the information, good luck with your prospectin'."

The two men stood, and Abner said, "Son, I hate to see one so young, so driven by hate and bound for vengeance. I think you know what the Scripture says about forgiveness so I won't cross biblical swords with a preacher's son, but don't forget that Hebrews 10:30 says *Vengeance belongeth unto me, I will recompense, saith the Lord.* Now, I don' mean to be preachin' at'chu, but all I gots to read is an ol' Bible I got from muh dear departed mother, so I spout it ever now an' then, 'sides, I been down that vengeance road and it ain't good travelin'. So, just think about it some, and remember what the Good Book says, that's God's job, not yourn." He chuckled and slapped Cord on the back as he walked them back to their horses. The two partners stood side by side as they watched their two visitors ride from their camp and cross the creek.

Dusk had lowered its curtain when Cord and Bird turned to the trail that followed the north fork of Chalk Creek, bound for TinCup, but first they needed a dry camp for the night. They rode into the dim light of the setting sun, although the golden orb had already been tucked away for the night, the glow of the last light of dusk made shadows of the distant horizon. Cord looked to the edge of the dark timber, saw a bit of a clearing and started to stop but Bird said, "No, not safe!" as she pointed up the steep slope of the almost bare mountainside. "There was an avalanche and maybe a rockslide here. We must go on, where the face is not so steep, and we have the cover of the trees."

She reined up about a hundred yards past the remains of the avalanche, nodded to the trees and a slight clearing just inside the tree line. She pointed to the creek that hugged the tree line, and said, "Water close, trees give cover, no rockslide."

"Suits me, I ain't anxious to get buried in a pile of rocks!" chuckled Cord, feeling a bit tired after the long day. He stepped down, took the reins from Bird and took the horses and mule to water while she started to prepare the cookfire. As he stood between the horses, he saw the shadowy wings of a golden eagle that circled overhead, curious as to the interlopers into his domain. Cord chuckled, shook his head, and mumbled, "Everybody's curious about us bein' here!"

4

ALPINE

THE SUN WAS AT THEIR BACK WHEN THEY RODE FROM THEIR high country camp to continue their trek westward. Bird and Cord rode side by side, the shadows stretching out before them, and the mountains rising beside them. Black timber was their constant companion, the skirts of which flared on either side of the little creek that was now little more than a trickle, scarcely wide enough for a short man to step over with one stride. But the alpine vegetation shouldered the little creek, soaking up the scarce sunshine and bending their short necks with multicolored blossoms to greet the rising sun.

The trail rose continually for a little more than a mile from their camp, and appearing as a massive broad barrier, stood a long blue-grey ridge totally devoid of any greenery, that blocked their way west, with every notch, gulley, and ravine painted white with the remaining snow drifts from the deep snows of winter. The north slopes of the mountains, though blanketed with black timber, snow showed among the trees covering the entire slope. But the trail bent to the north and cut into the timber, following a treeless draw that fell from the mountains to the north and showed a saddle that cradled the trail and offered an escape from the mountain lined valley. Another blue-grey peak crested just west of the saddle, but the talus slopes on either side stretched back from the valley like curtains withdrawn by the hand of the Creator.

They broke from the trees to a basin of multicolored carpet made up of the many low-growing alpine plants, many showing their colorful blossoms of lavender, blue, yellow, and reds. A cluster of lavender columbines with their delicate blossoms waved in the cool breeze of the high country, and on the far side of the trail a bed of bright orange paintbrush nodded as they passed. Yet where there was color, there was the constant reminders of the high country with lances of white stabbing down from the peaks and laying in the ice-carved ravines, crusted drifts refusing to release their hold on the mountains, yet slowly yielding to the bright sun and letting little trickles of snowmelt sneak from under their capes of white to feed the mountain streams and carve their way to lower climes. As they neared the crest of the pass, random bristlecone pines stood, their branches all pointing south while their north barks show red from windburn, and their trunks had yielded to the constant winds, leaning to the south as if trying to escape.

Clumps of darker green and blue-green shrubs lifted their heads above the lichen carpet, tenaciously holding to the loose soil of the land that stretched above timberline. Upthrust slabs of limestone displayed the orange and blue lichen and moss that decorated the flat rocks, while white blossoms with red freckles of the sandwort pushed against a bed of thick blooming Forget-me-not that boasted their blue blossoms. Further on the purple sky pilot lifted its thick blossoms to stand a little taller than the bright pink primrose. Cord was busy looking about, often standing in his stirrups to see a little further, a little more, but at the admonition of Bird, he avoided the icy crusted drifts and passed the cuts in the broad-shouldered mountains. He paused, again standing in his stirrups and sucked in the cool, almost cold, mountain air, thin though it was, and reveled in the endless beauty that surrounded them.

Everywhere they turned, an abundance of wildflowers strutted their colors, from the ground-hugging lichen to the tall standing purple, white and blue, red, and orange blossoms of the many unnamed flowers. As they topped the saddle crest of the pass, they stopped, stepped down and found a seat on a flat chunk of limestone and savored the beauty. Well above timberline, they were more than two miles above sea level and the air was thin but clear and fresh. At their feet was a reddish brown clump of haircap moss, that seemed to wave at the visitors with their hairy tentacles and shadowy forms.

Cord looked at Bird, "I've never known there was such beauty in the land." He pointed to the distant west where mountains stretched beyond their sight, mountains layered upon mountains, "Wherever we look, there's mountains and more. It's hard to realize such beauty could harbor such evil as the men we're chasing."

"But it is good to see the beauty even when there is

such evil," surmised Bird, laying her hand on Cord's. "I believe the Creator has brought us here to see what He has done."

Cord dropped his eyes to their hands, "I know, I know. I've been thinking too much about vengeance and not enough about forgiveness, but..." he shrugged and added, "I just have a hard time even thinking about forgiving them for what they've done. Every time I lay awake, the last images of my family come before me as if they are telling me to mete out justice to the outlaws that did that evil."

Cord stood, looked to the north down the long valley that was sided on the east by peaks well above timberline and on the west by a long bald limestone ridge. The trail followed a little creek that fed into a placid lake that lay in the quiet of the basin between the mountains. The crystal clear lake was about a half-mile long and less than a quarter-mile wide, and even though there was a bit of a breeze, nary a ripple showed on the surface of the mirror-like lake.

The trail took them over the little creek and hugged the lower end of the talus slope that came from the steep mountain sides on the east of the lake. They stopped beside the still water, stepped down and enjoying the shade of some tall spruce, they decided to have a nooning and rest the horses and mule that were breathing hard from the high altitude. Cord looked at the still water, saw a trout jump and splash as it caught a mayfly for its lunch. Cord grinned, looked at Bird, "Would you like some fish for dinner?"

"Fish would be good. Do you think you can catch some?"

Cord chuckled, "Oh, now, that's a challenge I can't

refuse!" and went to the packs for his fishing tackle. At the edge of the water he cut a nice willow, tied on the line and with a spade dug some worms and went to the water's edge. And the fish were hungry! In a short while, Cord had landed four nice cutthroat native trout and after a quick cleaning, proudly brought them to Bird and said, "Your turn!" and handed them off.

Bird smiled, rolled the cleaned fish in the cornmeal and dropped the first two in the pan that was waiting at fire's edge, and the sizzling and popping of the grease tantalized the hungry travelers. While the fish were frying, Cord stripped the gear from the horses and mule, let them have a roll in the dirt and tethered them within reach of water and grass and returned to the campfire for dinner.

They sat back in the shade under the big ponderosa, each holding a cup of hot coffee, as they savored the moment of full bellies and contentment with their place in life. Cord looked at Bird, "You know, it ain't right that we should be travelin' together, you know, us not bein' hitched."

"Hitched?" asked a frowning Bird.

"Yeah, you know, married, or like your people say, joined."

Bird smiled, leaned a little closer, "Do you want to be joined?"

Cord sighed heavily, "I've thought about it. I was thinkin' how I'm not havin' a hard time with the idea of finding those outlaws and bringing justice on 'em..."

Bird interrupted with, "That is a vengeance quest."

Cord frowned, looked sidelong at Bird, "vengeance quest?"

"Yes, when a warrior of my people has been

wronged, he spends time in prayer, then goes on a vengeance quest to make things right, back in balance. A vengeance quest, to search for vengeance for the wrong," explained Bird, smiling at Cord.

"A vengeance quest, huh? Sounds better when you explain it," he chuckled, then grew sober, "but the idea of ridin' with a woman that's not my wife and it not sittin' well. Reckon it's the preaching of my father and the teaching of my mother. She used to always say, 'Now Cordell, when it comes time for you to be lookin' for a wife, you mind how you treat her and always respect her for who she is and what she believes. And don't go forgettin' what the Good Book says about *a man leave father and mother and shall cleave to his wife and they twain shall be one flesh (Mt.19:5-6) and in Hebrews 13:4 Marriage is honorable in all, and the bed undefiled: but whoremongers and adulterers God will judge.'* She would always reach over and pat my knee, and add her own words, 'You'll make some woman a good husband.'" Cord shook his head, grinning. "Yeah, they had a lot to say about a man and a woman not being together unless they were married, and once married, that was for life!"

"Among my people, the joining is sometimes arranged between the father and the man, and the man gives gifts, you know, horses, weapons, other things, to pay the price of a woman." She dropped her eyes, remembering, then looked up at Cord, "My father would not listen to any man that came, he said it is not the way to do. He said among his people..."

Cord frowned and turned to face Bird, "What do you mean, among his people?"

"My father was White..."

"I know, you told me his name was White Eagle, was he not of your people, the Caputa?"

"My father was white, like you. He was not of my people the Caputa, he came from far away, he said he was of the Celtic People. That is why he was different and believed different about a man and a woman. But among my people, there are times when the woman and man choose each other and are joined with the blessing of their families. But because I was not of their people, the Kiowa did not allow me to be taken by a man. I had to obey the woman that I served." She stood and walked into the sunlight, spread her arms wide and lifted her face to the sun, smiling, and with eyes closed, said, "That is why I choose you."

"Choose me?" asked Cord, surprised at her comment.

Bird turned to look at Cord, smiling, "Yes. I chose you and came with you. When you are ready, we will be joined and be as a man and a woman together. That is what my father, White Eagle, did when he came to my people and found my mother."

Cord stood, walked closer to Bird, and grinning, said, "Don't I have anything to say about it?"

"No," answered Bird, smiling and walking away to fetch the horses and get ready to leave. Cord stood staring after her, shook his head, and followed.

The trail followed the creek that came from the little mountain lake and bent to the west, taking the easier way out of the higher mountains. The timber was thick, but the trail was good and easily followed and soon the timber thinned, and the creek showed itself in the bottom of the draw, beaver ponds and willows abundant. But on the far side, Cord noticed the creek had pushed its way through the bottom of a talus slope, carving its way through the rocky soil and carrying with it the silt and more. They rode another mile or so and were stopped by the sight of a man busy at a rocker box, but he was also staring at the two riders before him. A rifle lay on the man's lap, the muzzle pointed their direction.

Cord called out, "We're friendly!" with one hand lifted high and palm showing as the other held the reins and lead rope of the mule. "Alright if we come closer?" Cord called.

The man grunted, nodded and motioned them close, his one hand busy rocking the box and the other grasping the grip of the rifle. Cord nudged Kwitcher a little closer, dropped his free hand and crossed his arms over the pommel of his saddle as he leaned forward. "We're Cord Beckett and Yellow Singing Bird. We come from over the hill, visited with Abner and John, they told us about a few men over here prospecting. We're not lookin' for anything but information." He paused, and at the nod of the man, continued, "Been lookin' for some brigands, call themselves Bushwhackers or Red Legs, mighta been through here a while back. Seen anyone like that?"

"Why?" grunted the prospector.

"Well, they done some raidin' and killin' back east, and I've been after 'em ever since. They need a little justice brought to 'em."

"You gonna do that all by yore lonesome?"

"That's the idea."

The man who appeared to be middle-aged with a full beard, thick eyebrows, matted hair that hung from the floppy felt hat, and wearing a homespun shirt tucked into homespun britches that were tucked into tall boots, finished with the load on the rocker, stood with the rifle in hand, looking at Cord and Bird, then said, "Yeah, they was some o' them through here, early spring, din't stay long. They was caught goin' through a cabin, took ever'thin' and shot the man, name of Jim Lotts. He recovered, back at work. They din't get no gold, ain't none of us got much, an' they left. Jim said he thought they went downstream to the park, coulda gone anywhere from there. Ain't been back, though..." he shrugged, and continued, "...but you know, I heard tell of some other newcomers, but they sounded like the same ones, but don't rightly know." He looked up at Cord, "Step down, it's gettin' late. We don' get many visitors 'roun chere, 'specially wimmen." He looked from Cord to Bird, back to Cord, "She cook?" he asked.

Cord frowned, looking at the man, "She cooks for me sometimes. Why?"

"I got me some fresh meat. Kilt a moose an' got it hangin'. A good cook can do wonders with moose meat. I'll share it wit'chu if'n she cooks us up some."

Cord looked at Bird who was grinning, then smiled and nodded. "I like moose meat."

The man grinned, nodding, extended his hand and said, "My name's Jim Taylor. Been 'roun these parts a few years. There ain't too many of us, but we get together now'n then." He motioned for Cord and Bird to follow as he started to the trees.

Well hidden in the trees, a log cabin began to show itself and Jim walked to a hanging metal triangle and grabbed a metal rod and began to ring the triangle. He paused, rang it again, paused and rang it again. He grinned as he looked at a bewildered Cord and Bird,

"That's the dinner bell when I ring it like that. There'll be four or five other hungry men come for their fair share." He looked at Bird, "Oh, we'll help you, don'chu worry none. We like to get together ever now'n then, eat, tell lies, swap stories, you know how it is with lonely men." He chuckled as he turned toward Bird, pointed to a ring of stone with some firewood stacked nearby and a stack of pans and a coffee pot with a piece of canvas covering them.

Bird smiled, looked at Cord, "While you tend to the animals, I'll get started." She looked at Jim, "Got'ny coffee?"

"Yes ma'am!" declared Jim, moving to the door of the cabin and disappearing.

5

SOURDOUGHS

Bird had made a habit of picking edibles along the way and now dug into her dinner pouch, as she called it, and began filling the big pot with cattail shoots, amaranth, onion, yampa and sego lily. Some of the men watched, frowned, but as the pot began to cook with the two big rump roasts from the moose, their bellies began to grumble and their mouths watered in anticipation of the rare feast they were about to enjoy.

As the men wandered into camp, they approached Cord with frowns, but willingly extended their hands and introduced themselves as Jim Taylor stood beside him and made the introductions. Five men gathered near the fire, exchanged small talk about their diggings, spoke softly, a little wary of the visitors. The prospectors were a cautious lot, and Cord looked around at the men who made up this little group. Jim seemed to be a leader, or at least one of the old-timers, compared to the relative newcomers, and the rest were Fred Lotts, a loner, quiet man, but with watchful eyes, never missing a thing. Ben and Charlie

Gray, brothers, worked their sluice together and this was their second year, Fred and Carl Siegel were also brothers, but they had independent claims and used rocker boxes.

Jim spoke up and asked, "Anybody seen those two from south of the border?"

"You mean the Mex's?" asked Fred Siegel. "Ain't seen 'em fer a while, couple days or so, they've been pannin' the creek, lookin' fer color. Last I seen of 'em they was gettin' down near the park."

Jim turned to Cord to explain, "Willow Creek runs northwest and the park is a big basin that sits in the middle of the different mountain ranges. It's 'bout eight miles by fifteen or so, got some timber, little creeks, all feedin' into the bigger Taylor River that runs south outta here. There's a good creek, Texas Creek, that comes from the back side of the Sawatch Range and cuts through the park. A few have panned it, but nobody's showed any color that I know about."

"They mighta been too far away to hear the dinner bell!" offered Ben Gray, who was answered by the laughter of the others, but Fred Lotts growled, "I ain't never too far away to hear the dinner bell!"

Bird nodded to Cord who motioned to Jim, "Looks like dinner's ready! Ever'body bow your head so I can pray 'bout it!"

A surprised Cord glanced to Bird and back to Jim, bowed his head and listened as Jim began, "Lord, we're grateful for the time together and the visitors..." and finished with a thank you and an amen. He lifted his head with a smile and grabbed a plate and a cup and started the line. Everyone joined the line, all anxious for the woman cooked meal.

As they sat around eating, Cord asked, "The two that are missing, have they been around a while?"

"They came through here last fall, then came back this spring. They seem to be hard workers, know what they're doin', but as far as I know, they have yet to show color," explained Jim, getting nods of agreement from the others. "The older one, Manuel, uh, Rodriguez is his last name I think, seems to be the one that knows more 'bout prospectin'. He kinda orders the younger one, who is also a bit smaller, around. I think his name is Juan Martinez. Don't know if they're related or not." He looked to Fred, "Didn't they build 'em a cabin?"

"Yeah, looks to be well built, not very big, but ample. Peak roof, split 'em some shingles, so..." he shrugged. Shingles were a rarity for mountain cabins, especially among prospectors who don't want to take the time to split shingles and make that type of roof, choosing a slant sod roof for their temporary shelter. Building does not make money, prospecting does.

Fred added, "It's on the east side of the creek, back in the trees, but easy to see."

Cord frowned as he thought of the isolated couple of prospectors, wondering if they were alright or not, and asked Jim, "Have they ever come to one of your dinner-bell gatherings?"

"Oh yeah, they have. This is the first time anyone has missed out, but no one's obligated, it's just a break in the monotony, a time to share a kill, like the moose I got, and such." He shrugged as he watched the others going to their horses and readying to leave.

The last light of day was quickly fleeing the mountain vale and the men were anxious to get back to their cabins for the night. With a wave as they left, the others rode away from Jim's cabin and Cord and Bird, retreated to the camp laid out by Cord just back in the trees beyond Jim's cabin. He had laid out a bit of a fire and when they came back into the clearing, Cord stuck a lucifer and started the fire, not that they needed the warmth or the light, it was just something to dispel the night and make for a more comfortable camp.

A pair of lonesome coyotes began their chorus, prompting the night hawks to add their shrill high-pitched peents, but the one that got their attention was the cry and bark of a cougar, making the horses restless and getting the mule's attention.

Cord looked at Bird, asked, "What was that?"

Bird looked at Cord with an intense expression as she drew near, glancing to the trees and back to Cord, "Cougar! Some call them mountain lion, or catamount. A big cat!"

"I've heard of 'em, never seen one, are they dangerous?"

"They can be, they can kill a horse, a man..." she shrugged, moving a little closer when the cat screamed again.

Cord reached for another stick, tossed it into the fire, rose to his feet and went to the pack to retrieve his Sharps rifle. His Henry was already near his blankets, but the Sharps was a bigger, more powerful weapon, although a single shot. He checked the pickets of the animals, wanting them secure, but also able to break loose in the event of being attacked. He knew the mule would be more of a fighter, and maybe Kwitcher, but he was not too sure about Bird's appaloosa. The animals were tethered close to the camp, the fire visible to them and Bird had moved their blankets closer to the fire.

Both Cord and Bird were careful not to stare at the fire, wanting to preserve their night vision that would be ruined by looking directly at the bright light of the fire.

Another scream from the night sounded a little closer and Cord looked at Bird, "Either he's movin' pretty good, or there's two of 'em."

"It is usually a big tom that prowls at night, but they are most often alone. Although I have heard stories of more than one moving together."

"Oh, that's encouraging," replied Cord, checking the load in the Sharps, laying it against the log they used for a bench, then picked up his Henry and checked the loads, jacking a round in the chamber and carefully lowering the hammer. He set it beside the Sharps, looked to Bird's blankets on the far side of the fire, saw her rifle lying beside and on the edge of her blankets and nodded to the woman.

They went to their blankets, but both lay awake, staring into the darkness of the trees, listening to every sound of the night. The common sounds of the nighthawk, chirps of the many smaller birds, and other sounds seemed to fall quiet. Although not unusual for the darkness to silence the animals of the forest, for complete silence to descend was uncommon. Even the wail of the coyotes, or the howl of the wolves, were silent, but the scream and huffing cough of the cougar sounded even closer.

The horses stood tense, heads up, ears pricked, as they sidestepped nervously. The mule stood still, but he too had his head uplifted and ears tall, eyes wide. When the scream came again, their heads shifted as one, looking into the darkness of the trees, nostrils flaring and their nervousness evident.

Cord came to his feet, Sharps in hand, his back to the low fire as he searched the shadows of the trees, watching for any giveaway of the presence of the cougar. He turned slowly, searching the trees around the camp, as Bird also came to his side, rifle in hand. They stood back to back, watching the trees, listening for the slightest sound, glancing to the animals for any indication of the presence of the Cougar. Blue was at Cord's side, pivoting with his master, and a low growl came as he leaned forward, one forefoot lifted, head low, hackles raised. His growl came a little louder and he was frozen in place, staring at the trees, apparently seeing something Cord did not.

He whispered to Bird, "I think Blue sees something."

"Yeeooowww, yeeow," came a scream that made both Cord and Bird jerk, but the animals did not move, although the mule lowered his head a little, still staring into the night.

Cord and Bird stood back to back and were reassured by the touch of one another, but a sudden jerk by Bird as she stepped away, gasped, and lifted her rifle, startled Cord, but he did not move, watching the trees as the growl of Blue sounded louder and the dog stepped forward. Bird fired her rifle, jacked another round, fired again, both shots coming almost simultaneously, followed closely by the bray of the mule. Cord started to turn, but Blue lunged forward, growling and barking, and Cord saw the flash of tawny fur, lifted his big Sharps and dropped the hammer on the target as it lunged for the big stallion. The bullet took the cougar in the shoulder, driving it to the ground, but it squirmed, growling, fighting to get to his feet, and Kwitcher jerked free of his tether and charged the downed cat just as Blue sunk his teeth in the back of the neck of the catamount. Kwitcher reared up, eyes wide and crazed, and drove his front feet into the ribs and head of the downed cougar.

Cord grabbed his Henry, glanced to Bird and saw another cougar on the ground, turning and slapping at the air as the mule charged, teeth bared, head lowered, ears back and screaming. The lion drew back, but the mule sunk his teeth in the flank of the cat who whirled around, just as Bird fired her Henry, the bullet blossoming blood in the neck of the big cat. Cord turned back to the fight between the cat, the dog, and the stallion, but saw the cat had lost the fight, probably due to the big .52 caliber slug from the Sharps that broke the beast's shoulder and drove into its heart.

Within moments, the fight was over, but the animals were still tense and nervous, prancing in place, and Cord grabbed up the leads of both the stallion and the mule, comforting them with a low voice and his reassuring touch. He picketed them again, and with Blue at his side, and Bird still watching with rifle in hand, Cord reached for the first cat, started to pull it away from the camp and the voice of Jim Taylor came near,

"What's happenin'?" He stepped into the light of the fire, a rifle in hand. Bird looked at the man, "Visitors," motioning to the bloody carcasses of the cougars.

"Two of 'em?" he asked, incredulous. "Ain't never heard of two of 'em huntin' together!" he declared, as he went to Cord's side to help him drag the carcasses away. He chuckled, "Musta smelled that fine supper Bird cooked. Guess they was lookin' for leftovers!"

6

PREY

THE MAIN TRAIL RODE A SHOULDER OF THE TIMBER-COVERED flats while the bed of Willow Creek took the low ground at the foot of the steep shoulders of the mountains that marked the east edge of the valley. The sun was struggling to bend its morning rays over the timber-covered buttes, and shone as long golden lances stabbing at the scattered clouds overhead as Cord and Bird rode from their camp, glad to put the restless night behind them, although Bird insisted on skinning out the catamounts and taking the pelts with them.

"If we can stop a little early, I'll flesh out and soak the hides, and we'll have some very good leather. Do you want to leave the fur on, or just have the leather?" asked Bird, glancing to Cord who rode beside her.

"Oh, I dunno, whatever you think and whatever you want to use 'em for," shrugged Cord, and continued, "I ain't never had to worry 'bout cougar hides before."

"It makes a very soft leather, good for many things.

And the talons will make a fine necklace for my man," she smiled as she cast a coy smile to Cord.

Cord frowned, looked past Bird and stood in his stirrups, pointing to the east and the creek bottom, "That's smoke, and more than just a cookfire. Jim said those two Mex had their camp 'bout there. Might be trouble!" he declared as he reined Kwitcher to cut through the timber.

Willow Creek meandered through a low draw thick with willows and more. The ripples in the creek sent the water crashing through the valley bottom, with the mountains standing faraway in the west. The shoulder of the long plateau on the east edge stood no more than twenty feet above the white water that cascaded over the rocky bottom, and it was in the pine thickets on the east edge that smoke lazily spiraled into the early morning light. The smell of smoke and the quiet of the woods puzzled Cord and Bird, but they pushed through the oftentimes thick woods toward the source of the smoke. A small clearing held what had been a crude cabin erected recently, but now was black with burnt logs and swirling smoke. The cabin had faced the shoulder of the creek bottom, but the only thing marking the doorway was the sprawled body of a man. The stench of burnt flesh filled the clearing, prompting Cord and Bird to cover their faces with neckerchiefs.

They stepped down, ground-tied the animals and walked slowly around the cabin. Cord knelt down beside the prostrate body and reached to feel for a pulse, but a groan surprised him, and he sat back, looking aghast at the prone figure. "Juan, Juan, where..." moaned the man, trying to crawl as he dug his fingers in the dirt.

"It's alright, we're here to help," said Cord, slowly rolling the man to his back. His face was blackened, his hair singed, his clothing had burnt, and raw flesh showed on his thighs. Scared eyes looked at Cord as he struggled to speak, "My nephew, Juan, where...?"

"We're looking for him now," answered Cord as he stood and bent to grasp the man under his arms and pull him away from the smoldering ruins. "Who did this?" asked Cord, looking down at the man as he dragged him away from the smoldering ruins.

"Bush..." was all the man could say, as he struggled to breathe.

Cord nodded to Bird, motioned with his chin to the remains of the cabin as if to tell her to look for the other man as Cord pulled the burnt body away. It was just a couple yards to the tree line and shade, and as Cord lay the man down, he looked up at Cord, frightened eyes saying what he could not mutter, and the last breath of life whispered from the charred figure. No movement, no breath, and only sightless eyes told the tale of the dead man. Cord stood and looked toward the cabin's remains, but Bird shrugged her shoulders and shook her head to tell what she had found or not found.

Cord glanced to the body, stepped away and walked to where Bird stood, looking about.

When Cord neared she said, "It looks like maybe a body there in the corner, but..." she shrugged.

He spotted two picks, two spades, a metal pan, and glanced from the prospecting tools to the trail that led to the creek below, saw many tracks of horses and he knelt to look at the tracks. He glanced up to Bird, "Looks like they had comp'ny, near as I can tell at least three on horseback." He stood, pointed to the tracks and said, "The footprints show three also, and blood there," he pointed to spots of blood on the ground near the stoop of the cabin, "says they musta shot these two, and took ever'thing they could."

Cord walked to the stack of tools, grabbed up a spade and went to where the body of the one man lay and began to dig a grave. Bird found the remnant of a blanket and went to the cabin and put together what she could of the other man, boots, a few bones, pieces of canvas britches, and little else.

She wrapped them in the blanket and went to where Cord was digging, laid the bundle beside the body and said, "I'm going down to the creek, see if there is anything else."

Cord nodded and continued his digging.

As Cord shoveled the last of the dirt over the bodies, Bird came up the trail from below, Blue leading the way having enjoyed the hike with the woman. His tongue lolled out the side of his mouth as he bounded to Cord's side, rubbing up against him.

Cord sat back on a rock, wiped the sweat from his brow and looked at Bird as she began, "Those two had at least one rocker box, other tools, all broken to pieces. The tracks of the horses led up the trail to the cabin, where they apparently done their best to destroy everything. But they didn't find these..." she grinned as she lifted the hem of her tunic and lifted two pouches from her waistband. "I looked around as if I was the one digging, looked for a likely spot and saw a flat rock beside a big boulder, lifted it, and there they were!"

Cord frowned, motioned Bird closer and she sat beside him after handing over the two pouches, which were quite heavy. Cord sat one down, pulled the drawstring on the other and poured out some gold dust into the palm of his hand. He grinned as he returned the dust to the pouch, looked at Bird, "I'm thinking Manuel and Juan were smarter than the Bushwhackers. Or maybe they had another stash the Bushwhackers got and were mad there wasn't more."

"So, what do we do with this?"

"There's nothing left," began Cord, nodding to the ruins, "nothing that says where they were from or where there was any family. So, we'll just hang onto it until we find out more about 'em. They probably have family somewhere, but where?" shrugged Cord, rising to go to the horses. As they mounted, he looked at Bird, "I'm thinkin' we need to tell the others what happened here, cuz it looks like the raiders went thataway," pointing to the trees and a little trail that split the pines, "and the rest of 'em are upstream from here, but they need to be wary, so, let's go there first. Then we'll decide what else we need to do, maybe track those outlaws and see where they went or where they're going. They could be some of the men I'm after."

"You mean, *we're* after," added Bird, grinning as she mounted her appaloosa.

They rode up the trail that sided the stream bed of Willow Creek, expecting to find some of the other prospectors and give them a warning about the bushwhackers in the area. The first diggings they came to was the loner, Fred Lotts. He heard them coming, rose from his rocker box with rifle in hand and as they neared, he growled, "What'chu want? You ain't welcome here!"

Cord held up one hand, they were opposite Lotts' diggings on the far side of the creek and he called out,

"Just wanted to let you know, your neighbors, the two Mexicans, were hit by bushwhackers! They killed both of 'em but cleaned 'em out, burnt their cabin. We buried them together in the clearing beside the cabin. Thought you oughta know."

"How'd you know they was bushwhackers?"

"Manuel told me that with his last breath, he had been shot, and was badly burned but crawled out of the cabin. Juan didn't make it out. The outlaws burnt the cabin, destroyed his rocker and everything else they could. From the tracks, looks like there were three of 'em, but they headed out to the north."

Lotts nodded, shook his head, said nothing more and watched as Cord and Bird rode away, then returned to his own rocker but kept his rifle within reach. Cord knew the man would be a little on the nervous side but watchful and more careful after the news of the attackers. But there was nothing else he could do except to warn the others.

The Gray brothers and the Siegel brothers were upstream from Fred Lotts and took the news about the same, asked a few questions that Cord could not answer but told them, "We'll be trackin' 'em a ways, just to see where they went. If their trail turns back thisaway, we'll try to get a warning to you, but just be ready, no matter what."

The men nodded and turned back to their work as they watched Cord and Bird ride away. Jim Taylor's diggings were to the south side of the creek where the creek moved east to west and bent around the low-rising butte. Taylor's diggings were in the face of the butte above the creek, and he had a chute that carried his ore down closer to the creek where he had a sluice box and would wash the ore at the end of each day. He pushed his handmade wooden wheelbarrow from the mouth of the mine to dump it into the chute, spotted Cord and Bird coming near and stopped, stood with hands on hips above them and called down, "I thought you two left!"

"We did!" answered Cord, reining up to lean on the pommel of his saddle and look up to Taylor, shading his eyes in the doing. He called up and started to tell his tale, but Taylor motioned he was coming down and as he slid down the diggings, Cord and Bird stepped down to wait.

After they shared the news of the Bushwhackers, Taylor asked, "Didn't you say that was who you were after?"

Cord nodded, "Ummhmm, but I don't know if it's the same bunch. We reckon to track 'em a ways, see where they're headed and then decide."

"Wal, if it looks like they be comin' this way, be sure to git here 'fore they do an' give us a warnin'!"

Cord grinned, "Will do!" then swung back aboard Kwitcher, gave Blue the high sign and he and Bird turned their mounts back to the trail to resume their original journey.

7

SLAUGHTERHOUSE

TAYLOR TURNED BACK TO HIS SLUICE, STOPPED AND DROPPED to one knee, stretching out his hand to look at the ground before him. A trail followed the creek upstream to the confluence of Willow Creek and what most were calling West Willow. The fresh tracks of several horses showed in the dirt, and Taylor frowned, realizing he had not noticed the tracks when he came to work earlier in the day.

He stood, turned to holler at Cord, "Hey, wait up!" and when Cord turned, he waved them over.

As they crossed the shallow creek, Taylor followed the tracks just a short ways, turned back and pointed to the trail before him and said to Cord, "Those tracks weren't there this mornin' when I came o'er. Musta passed when I was in the diggin's."

Cord slipped to the ground, knelt beside the trail and examined the tracks, glanced back to Bird, "They're the same. They musta crossed over downstream and came up this side." He turned to look at Taylor as he stood, "Where does this trail go?"

"Dunno for sure. Ain't never followed it. Been too busy with muh diggin's to go explorin'. I reckon it follers the West Willow up through Slaughterhouse Gulch," he shrugged, sticking his thumbs behind his galluses and looking at Cord. "You gonna foller 'em?"

Cord nodded, glanced up the trail and mounted up, waved to Taylor and started up the trail, Bird close behind.

Pine and spruce blanketed the flanks of the higher mountain to the west of West Willow Creek, but the eyebrow trail followed the creek upstream for about a half-mile until they came to the confluence of West Willow and a smaller no-name creek. This was as far as Taylor had explored but he told Cord that when smaller creek joined, the upstream of the smaller no-name creek cut through Slaughterhouse Gulch. Cord stopped, leaned on the pommel as he looked upstream of the little creek and could see the narrow trail cutting through the trees. He looked upstream, turned to look at Bird, shook his head and dropped into his saddle to resume their search.

But Bird called out, nudged her appaloosa closer and asked, "What are we going to do?"

"Well, Taylor said Fred Lotts had followed this trail and that it comes out into the same park that sits below their diggin's on the Willow. So, if it makes a circle, should be easy to follow and see where those outlaws are headed."

"Then what?"

"Dunno, guess I'll just have to see what happens."

Bird sat back in her saddle, looked at Cord and all about, thinking something but saying nothing. Gave a deep sigh, forced a smile and nodded for Cord to lead the way. Cord shook his head, wondering what she was thinking, not sure what he was thinking, but feeling the urge to continue to follow the outlaws, and try to determine if they were some of the same bushwhackers that killed his family. Just how he was going to do that, he did not know, but surrendered to the pull of vengeance anyway.

———

THE LITTLE CREEK soon petered out, but the trail kept to the tree line on the north of the long grassy park that carved a serpentine path to the west. With granite-tipped peaks in the distance, the timber-covered foothills of the lower climes covered the land beside the long park. As the trail followed the contours of the land and yielded to the shoulders of the hills, it crawled ever higher toward a saddle crossing that dropped them into an even narrower gulch with thicker timber and a trail that often had switchbacks to drop from the higher hills. After about five miles they broke from the timber, following a long finger ridge that pointed into a wide and long park. Cord reined up, looking about at what he guessed had been an ancient high-country lake, but now showed little more than the sandy bottom with deep silt and low grasses. As he looked about, it was evident where the high water mark had been, the timber stopped short as if cut back, and the low humps of timber-covered mounds appeared as ancient islands in the shallows of the big lake. But he could see no cut where the water would have drained, and he could only assume that the land had shifted and left the land-locked lake to eventually dry up and leave nothing but silt as a memory.

At the west end of the dry lake, a steep-shouldered hill rose high above, showing a bald top that could have been the cone of an ancient volcano but now showed only as a granite-topped hill. At the north end of the dry lake was the saddle and the trail that pointed northwest, probably the trail that would take them back to the Willow Creek basin.

Cord glanced to Bird, pointed to a grassy shoulder at the edge of the trees. "How 'bout we make camp here?"

Bird smiled, nodded, and nudged her appaloosa to the edge of the trees and quickly slipped to the ground. There was a little trickle of a spring-fed creek near the trees that would provide them sufficient water for their needs, and she quickly went to the pack mule to offload the bundle of catamount hides.

Cord said, "I'm gonna follow their trail a short ways, just to see what direction they're headed. I might see if I can get us some fresh meat too."

Bird smiled, nodded, and carried first one, then the other, bundle of hides to the edge of the little creek. "I'll work on these till you get back," she called as he started away.

Although they had passed a couple prospect holes as they rode through Slaughterhouse Gulch, there were no active diggings and they saw no one either camped or working. The trail they followed was an established trail, little more than a game trail, but the tracks of the outlaws stayed with the trail. When Cord left their camp to follow the trail a mite further, it was evident the outlaws were staying with the established route and when he stopped on a slight promontory, he stood in his stirrups and with his binoculars, he saw where the trail still hugged the tree line but cut across the open flat to a cut to the south of what he thought had been an ancient volcano. With the lighter green of aspen and the low-growing shrubbery, it was evident that cut carried water, and the outlaws had taken that trail, probably looking for fresh diggings and an easy target for their robbery.

With a glance to the lowering sun that made silhouettes of the distant peaks, Cord put his binoculars back in the case in his saddlebags, and started to turn back to camp, but movement at the edge of trees around the point of land, caught his attention. He carefully slipped the Sharps rifle from the scabbard, stepped to the ground, checked the load and started to the edge of the trees. As he suspected, some deer were tiptoeing from the woods toward the little creek, and he stepped behind a tall aspen and waited. When they were in the open, he picked his target, a young buck showing a two-point rack in the velvet, and with the tree as a leaning rest, he squeezed off his shot. The big Sharps .50 bucked and spat smoke, lead, and death, blossoming red on the low side of the buck, just behind his front leg, a definite kill shot.

The buck jumped and came down on limp legs into a heap, dead before he hit the ground. The others scampered away, taking cover in the trees and were soon gone. Cord chuckled, reloaded the Sharps and slid it into the scabbard, picked up the reins of Kwitcher and started toward his kill, his mouth already watering with the anticipated taste of fresh broiled venison steak.

———

THEY WERE JUST around the point of rocky ridge when the racketing of a rifle shot chased them into the steep draw that held Lottis Creek. They reined up, looked at one another, and the man in the lead, Charles 'one-eyed' Blunt growled, "Judd," as he pointed, "go back 'roun' that point, see if you can see who done that!"

The man known as Judd was Judd Pollack. He and his friend, Frank Witt, had joined up with Blunt after he made promises of riches by robbing solitary and unsuspecting prospectors, he told them, "The hills are full of dumb suckers that will do all the work, an' we can just take the pouches o' gold from 'em after they dig it up!"

It sounded easy, and so far they had found some, but not what he had promised. It seemed all they were doing was running from anyone that decided to chase after them and when they asked Blunt about the easy pickings, he just grunted and said, "We'll find 'em!"

Now they were getting jumpy every time they heard a rifle shot. Judd shook his head as he jerked the head of his mount around to go back on their trail to see who was shooting and if someone was on their trail.

As he rounded the point, he looked into the wide park of the dried lake bed, saw nothing, but decided to climb the slide rock slope of the hill beside him. He stepped down, ground-tied his mount, and started climbing the slide rock, using hands, knees, and pushing with his toes. He made it to the trees, turned, sat down, and looked across the lake bed, scanning the distant tree line where the trail they followed lay. He thought he saw movement, but without binoculars he could not be sure, but as he looked, watched, and waited, he determined it was a solitary man that had killed a deer and was loading the carcass on his horse. The man turned away and disappeared into the trees.

Judd was satisfied, slipped down the slide rock and mounted up to return to his companions and report. "It was just one man, kilt him a deer and went back in the woods!" he declared as he looked at the scruffy faced leader, Blunt. With a dirty black patch over one eye and heavy black whiskers and brow, he was a mean looking and acting creature and a man most others kept shy of, but Charles, Charlie Blunt was meaner than he looked and lived without conscience or concern for anyone but himself.

He grunted, jerked the head of his mount around and motioned the others to follow and they fell in line behind him. They were following this trail that was supposed to take them down to the Taylor River canyon where Blunt said he heard about some prospectors that had struck gold. Their purpose was to relieve those same prospectors of the extra burden of carrying those heavy gold pouches.

8

UNION CANYON

THE HAIR ON THE BACK OF HIS NECK PRICKLED, A SHIVER RAN down his spine, and Cord slipped to the far side of the carcass to look back at the flat of the park. Movement on the far side caught his eye and he stepped to his mount, slipped the binoculars from the case and using the cover of his mount, leaned on the saddle and rested his binoculars to look across the park at the opening of a deep draw at the base of the long ridge coming from the higher mount. Movement at the edge of the trees, showed a solitary figure, scanning the flats between them, a horse moved at the base, tethered and waiting for its rider.

Cord grinned, knowing this had to be one of the outlaws and they were watching their backtrail. They had originally started across this park, or dry lake bed, moving to the north and Cord thought they were bound for the valley of the Taylor River, but apparently they had cut back across the park, probably following the little creek that crossed in the scrub oak and willows and wound its way around the point of the talus slope at the mouth of that canyon. But if they were going that way, it would be best to wait until morning before trying to follow. Cord chuckled, watched as the man slid down the talus slope, swung aboard his mount and disappeared into the draw.

Cord returned to their camp to a smiling Bird who had laid in a cookfire that was just beginning to show flames as dusk began to drop its curtain over the little clearing they had chosen for their camp. She glanced to the little creek and the small dam she made to provide a pool of water to soak the hides, and Cord caught her glimpse, walked close and saw the handiwork of the woman as she prepared the hides in the customary way of her people.

He grinned at her, "So, what'chu gonna make outta them hides?"

"Oh, I have not decided yet. The leather will be soft and there are many things that could be made, like warm moccasins, or..." she shrugged with a coy smile. She had come to his side to help with offloading the carcass of the deer and they soon had backstrip steaks simmering over the fire. A pot of potato, osha, and yampa was also simmering on the coals, beside the coffee pot that had begun its dance on the flat rock pushed into the coals.

They enjoyed a leisurely supper, and after their coffee, Cord explained about the men they followed. "They've gone down a steep draw on the far side of the park yonder, and I'm thinkin' that prob'ly drops down to the Taylor River. After that, I dunno. I can't see 'em gettin' too far from likely prospectin' spots, so, we might follow 'em down that way a short distance, then decide. I'm thinkin' the most of 'em will be back thataway," nodding behind them toward the bigger Sawatch Range of mountains. "There's been more prospectin' and strikes o'er to the California Gulch and Oro City way and that'd be more to their likin'. But since there's only three of these, the bigger bunch mighta split up."

Bird sat quiet, looking at Cord as she glanced from her coffee cup to the fire and back to Cord. He could tell she was thinking, but not what. He dropped his eyes, thinking back on the events that had brought them this far, but mostly about the time when his family had been killed by the Red Legs or Bushwhackers and he watched helplessly from the trees. From that time to this, foremost in his mind was vengeance, justice, anything that might take the pain of his loss away. After spending the first years after the end of the war preparing himself to find the men who were guilty of the horrible act of murdering his family who had nothing to do with the war that was already over, and bring them to justice or at the very least find vengeance. But now he was questioning himself and his motives. Bird had accepted his quest and joined him, not because she wanted vengeance, but because she cared for him and wanted to stand beside him no matter what his choices might be or bring. Her presence had made him examine his motives and his purpose, even given him something different to dwell on, life without the vengeance quest, but could he give that up? Didn't the memory of his family demand that vengeance?

He looked away from the fire, sighed heavily and stood, tossed out the dregs of his coffee and said, "Let's turn in, we'll see what tomorrow brings with the sun."

Bird smiled and began the clean-up after their meal and to prepare for the coming night.

———

A LOW GROWL from Blue brought Cord instantly awake. He did not move but looked all about in the darkness. The deep shadows were outlined by the light from the full moon, showing the horses with heads up, ears pricked, and looking toward the edge of the trees and the wide park beyond. Cord slowly moved from his blankets, leaving them rumpled as if they still covered his form. A whisper of movement told him Bird also left her blankets. They both, with rifles in hand, moved into the deeper shadows of the tall fir and spruce. A quick glance to his right told him Bird was behind a big spruce with low branches spread wide, giving her ample cover.

Cord looked to the clearing of the camp, the cook-fire ring showed nothing but grey ashes, but suddenly fire stabbed the darkness as lances of flame blossomed from at least two rifles. As fast as the shooters could lever cartridges into the rifles, the thunder of rifle fire racketed through the trees, ricochet after ricochet twanged from the rocks of the fire ring. Horses whinnied and screamed as they tore loose from the tethers and crashed away through the trees. The mule lay his ears back and brayed as he bucked from the woods.

Cord and Bird returned fire, aiming just above the flames of the attackers' rifles. Cord heard one grunt and moan followed by the crashing of branches as he scored a hit on one of the shooters, but bark split and splintered by his head and thunder erupted from behind him. It felt like the mule kicked him in the back, causing him to stand and bend over backward as the pale light of the full moon split the dark branches and watched him fall to his back. The thunder of rifle shots faded, and darkness washed over him, and silence descended upon him like a heavy blanket.

Bright sunlight warmed his face and a wet tongue stirred Cord, forcing him to slowly open his eyes. Pain kicked him in the back as if a plow horse was standing on him. He stifled a groan and did his best to look around. He was lying face down in the dirt and pine needles, Blue was licking his face and whimpering. Cord slowly rolled to his back, wincing from the pain, looking around as he moved. He felt at his hip, felt his pistol still in the holster. It had been under him and whoever the shooters were, they apparently thought him dead and did not move him. A quick look showed his rifle was missing. As he searched the area, his first thought was for Bird, and he twisted to look where she had been and saw an unmoving form lying face down behind the big spruce that had been her cover.

He tried to muster what strength he had and crawled to her side, putting his hand to her neck and feeling the cold damp flesh. She did not move, was not breathing, and her form was cold, blood covered her back and soaked her tunic. Cord slowly shook his head, knowing she was dead, and mixed emotions began to stir within him. He had begun to believe he loved her and was thinking about taking her as his wife, and they were growing closer in their faith. She had accepted Christ as her Savior when they sat in on the worship service back at Fort Lyon and wanted to learn about the Christian faith, but now? Once again, he felt God had failed him and he was torn with emotions of loss, anger, revenge and more.

But he did not know if the attackers were still nearby or if they were gone, and he had to put his emotions aside and tend to his wounds and more. What about the horses? He knew if Kwitcher was free, being a one man horse with more loyalty than most, he would not be caught and would return, but he did not know about the mule or Bird's appaloosa. And what about their gear?

He put a hand to his back and felt the wetness of blood. He shook his head, moved closer to the trunk of the spruce, twisting around to sit up and evaluate his wound. Something would have to be done to stop the bleeding, and some type of bandage would be needed. He crawled to where their packs and saddles lay under the cluster of fir trees at the edge of the clearing. He was surprised to see the packs, but as he neared, it was evident they had been rifled and robbed. But he started sorting through the remains, believing any thieves would only take what they thought they could immediately use or anything of value. Bird's parfleche of medicinals and bandages had been searched, but most everything remained. Cord sighed heavily, knowing he not only needed the medicines and bandages, but he needed Bird's knowledge and skills. He smelled a couple smudges of ointment, recognized both the smell of onion and licorice and gathered up some cloth patches, smudged the ointment thickly and with wide bands of leather, crudely bandaged himself, the wound about elbow high on the right side of his back. He winced and struggled but was soon satisfied with his handiwork, knowing it would have to do for now.

Blue had stayed by his side and after struggling with the bandage, Cord was winded, but determined to look about to see what was left and what had been taken, trusting Blue to give a warning if any of the outlaws were near. Their gear, blankets and all were scattered about, but his saddle and the pack saddle remained as did Bird's saddle and blankets. He struggled to his feet, grabbed up a long stick to help support himself and he began gathering the gear together. He caught movement through the trees and quickly dropped behind a big spruce, bringing his pistol to bear, but the movement was Kwitcher, followed by the mule. Both were greeted by Blue, and they came into the clearing of the camp, trailing their leads beside them. Cord looked about, but the appaloosa was not to be seen.

Cord did his best to gather their gear together and was surprised to see the frying pan, coffee pot, and stew pot in a pile, the stew pot stomped on, and the handle of the frying pan broken off, but the coffee pot was undamaged, and it appeared the pans had been stacked together and were only stomped on and not moved. As he picked them up, thinking they could still be used, he saw a hump under the pine needles beneath the stew pot, and out of curiosity, knowing Bird was always the crafty one, he brushed away the needles to find the two pouches of gold taken from the camp of the burnt out Mexicans. Cord grinned, remembering the ways of the woman, and he glanced in the direction of her body, knowing she needed to be buried.

9

RESOLVE

IT WAS ALL HE COULD DO JUST TO MOVE AROUND THE CAMP, gathering the gear together, and more. But he had to take care of Bird before much of anything else. He forced himself to dig a grave, then wrap her body in the hides of the cougars and a blanket. He struggled to get her body into the grave, and had to stop and rest before continuing. He spent the time arguing with God, shaking his head at the turn of events and especially the loss of his woman, his partner, his friend. *First it's my family, and just when I thought I was getting things settled, You had to take Bird! Why?* He remembered a sermon of his father's that told of God's way, *For my thoughts are not your thoughts, neither are your ways my ways, saith the Lord.* Cord was troubled by those thoughts and tried to remember where that was found in the Scriptures.

He sat back against the tree trunk, pulled his saddlebags close and withdrew the Bible. He thought about his father's sermon and the book of Isaiah came to mind. He began flipping through the pages, saw notes in the margin and stopped at chapter fifty-five, frowned as he looked at a marked passage. The very passage he had remembered, verse 8, but as he looked, he frowned and shook his head, for at the top of the page, the last part of verse seven said, *let him return unto the Lord, and he will have mercy upon him; and to our God, for he will abundantly pardon.* Cord shook his head, took a deep breath and jammed the Bible back into his saddlebags, and began shoveling the dirt into the grave to cover the body of Bird.

It was almost the last shovel full of dirt that sent a stabbing pain into Cord's side, doubling him over. His hand went to the pain, and he felt the slight bulge and immediately knew what was the cause. The bullet that had driven into his back, had not exited and now was pushing against the muscle in his lower abdomen. It had to come out and the thought of cutting out the bullet caused Cord to shake his head, but he knew it could not be put off. He struggled to the fire pit, stirred the last of the coals and lay a couple sticks atop the grey ashes and coals. He stripped off his shirt and sat down on the big rock beside the fire. He lay his knife on the rock, the blade sticking into the edge of the flames. He placed Bird's medicine parfleche beside him, dug out some bandages and a poultice with her concocted balm, and with a deep breath, he reached for the knife and looked at the bulge in his lower stomach at his side.

After a bit of massaging, pushing, tugging, he felt he had the slug positioned where he could cut it out. With a deep breath, he reached for the knife, dipped it in the water to cool it, and lay the razor-sharp edge at the crest of the bulge in his side. He had already put the leather sheath in his mouth and now with another breath, he sliced open his own flesh, holding the bulge with his off hand and squeezing it to the surface. When the flesh cut opened, the slug was exposed, and he had to cut a little more to free the lead projectile. One more squeeze and it pushed out, enabling him to grab it and lay it aside. He took a deep breath as he placed the knife on the flat rock, the blade extending into the edge of the flame and as it began to glow orange, he bit down on the sheath, brought the hot blade to the wound, and cauterized the wound, screaming through the sheath as the hot blade burnt the flesh. He fell to the side, but had the consciousness to extend his hand with the knife away from his body.

He did not know how long he had been unconscious, but Blue lay at his side, watching over the prone form of his master. Cord reached out to his friend, stroked his head and said, "Thanks boy, you're the best."

He struggled to sit up, looking about, and then down to the wound. He shook his head and dragged the parfleche near. He gathered up the poultice, bandages, and wide strips of leather to fashion his bandage. He had to cover the more open wound at his back, and the fresh wound at his side, then wrap his middle with the leather to hold the bandages in place. Once finished, he put on his shirt, knowing he would need to find some food, for the outlaws had taken everything edible from his gear.

For the next three days, Cord kept busy just surviving. He had to drag the body of the one outlaw away from their camp and dumped it in a gulley and caved in the bank to cover it. He set snares for rabbits, bagged a couple sage hens with his pistol, and scrounged for any edibles like yampa, berries, cat tail shoots, Indian potato, and more. By the end of the third day, he felt he would be able to take to the trail the next morning and readied his gear before dark. He had scouted out the trail of the outlaws and before first light, he was on the trail.

The trail of the renegades crossed the edge of the big park, moving to the northwest and over a saddle. The track dropped from the ridge into the basin that lay below the trail that came from the camps at Tincup. From the crest of the saddle crossing, Cord looked to the northeast at the long stretch of granite-tipped peaks known as the Sawatch Range. They stood with shadowy faces as the slow-rising sun painted the back side of the mountains, casting long shadows across the park below. The massive mountains seemed to march together, making their way to the northwest, stretching out across the lower reaches of the country. Most of the mountains still held patches of snow on the granite peaks that stood above the skirts of black timber that covered the lower reaches, and the wide alluvial flat that lay before them.

It was a majestic scene and Cord stopped, leaned on his pommel and looked at the massive mountains, a scene he would never tire of enjoying. But the trail of the outlaws beckoned, and he nudged Kwitcher to the track that split the timber and dropped into the wide park below. As he broke from the timber, Cord reined up and looked over the park. It lay before him, a slight slope to the west, and stretched about six miles west to east, and about a mile and a half across. Willow Creek meandered from the hills to the east, while Taylor River came from the hills to the north, where they met, a small lake lay with its surface showing mirror-like and catching the first golden rays of sun as the big orb rose in the east and began painting the peaks of the mountains in a blaze of color.

The tracks of the outlaws took the game trail that lay just inside the tree line. Cord stepped down and examined the sign, noting there were four distinct sets of tracks. But there had been only three of the outlaws, one lay buried under the caved in ravine bank near the last camp. But there was one track, distinct from the others, that Cord recognized as those of the appaloosa that had been ridden by Bird.

The outlaws took to the trail that pointed to a long ridge that rode the edge of a wide and long alluvial plain made long ago. Islands of trees dotted the long plain that lay like a long narrow fan of soil washed down from the higher mountains, but the road climbed the hump of a hill in the middle, crossed the low swale and followed the west shoulder of the long ridge. As it moved east into the higher mountains, the trail followed the valley between the higher mountains that stood sentinel over the flats. When Cord crested the saddle crossing that would one day be called Cottonwood Pass and used as a stagecoach and wagon road, he paused and stepped down, looking at the gathering of mountain peaks that ran north and south. To the north lay the greatest number and tallest of the peaks of the Sawatch Range, and to the south was the beginning of that same range. Below him to the east, the trail cut through thick black timber that lay in the wide and long valley that separated the peaks to offer an escape for the runoff waters that would eventually feed the Arkansas River.

He was tired, and his wound was bleeding and needed attention. He mounted up, wincing with every movement, and pushed down to the timber and followed the pack trail to creek's edge and stepped down to make camp. He still had some of the fixings of Bird in the medicine parfleche and after tending to the animals and starting a small cookfire for the necessary coffee, he sat down on the rocky edge of the creek and began tending his wound.

Stripping off the old bandage, he put some of her balm on another pad of cloth, strapped in on the entry and exit holes of the wound and bound himself tightly, all the while thinking of Bird and trying to think of anything he could have or should have done to prevent her death, but his thoughts were fruitless. He shook his head, fighting his own emotions, both sorrow for the loss of the first woman he thought he loved, and anger at the ones that brought about her death. He gritted his teeth and took a deep breath, trying to clear his head and sort out the chores before him. First he needed to fix himself some food, then get some good rest, for he was determined to push on and find the outlaws that killed Bird, and he also believed they were part of the same bunch that had raided as Red Legs during the war and killed his family and burned the family farm.

10

———

GRANITE

HE STAYED ON THE TRAIL. EVEN WITH THE PAIN AND problems of the wound, he was determined to find the two outlaws that had struck their camp, stolen much of their gear, and killed Bird. He had never been this close to any of the former Red Legs, and he was determined to find them. He was into his third day on the trail when he came from the mountains and looked upon the wide stretch of flat land that lay in the Arkansas River Valley. A quick glance showed those he followed had turned away from the main trail that pointed east toward the river, and chose instead to turn to the north, keeping to the edge of the sparse trees that lay below the flanks of the Sawatch Range of mountains.

It was nearing the end of the third day when the shoulders of the mountains pushed toward the river and narrowed the passage. A huge talus slope stood imposing on the south bank of the river, rising over two hundred feet to stand tall over the river bottom, while on the north bank, the lower timber-covered hills shrank back in the shadows, allowing a wagon road to hug the shoulder as the river bent around the point. After a wide and lazy "S" curve with the river, the road pushed past another long canyon that carried another feeder creek, then into a narrower draw before opening to the settlement of Granite.

The town lay on both sides of the river with a rickety bridge crossing the fast moving waters. Although the river here was rather shallow, the water was cold and fast. But fortunately, on the near side stood both a livery and a tavern with an attached café. Cord reined up at the livery where a man sat in an armchair leaning against the big door, puffing on a pipe. He looked skeptically at Cord, nodded, as Cord asked, "Got room for muh animals?"

"Yup, cost you two bits each, but if'n you wanna sleep with 'em, it'll cost you another two bits."

Cord nodded, stepped down and followed the man into the big livery. They passed a cold forge and anvil that showed more dust than use, and the man walked with a limp to the back of the building, pointed to two empty stalls and nodded to the loft, "Hay up there."

But Cord had stopped at the stalls before those pointed at by the hostler. The pepper butt of the appaloosa had caught his attention, and he knew that was the gelding of Bird. He looked up at the hostler, led his animals to the stalls and asked the man, "The men that brought in that appaloosa, they still around?"

"Nope. They sold me that horse and that'n next to it. Took outta here this mornin'. Only stayed one night, an' I'm glad o' that. Got in a fight in the saloon, kilt a man o'er some cards. Took the pot and a bottle'n dared anyone to do anythin' 'bout it. We ain't got no sheriff no more, so..." he shrugged, shaking his head. He looked back at Cord, "They weren't friends o' your'n was they?"

"No."

"They was some mean hombres!" declared the hostler, stubbing his foot in the dirt at the memory of the night before.

"They say where they were goin'?" asked Cord.

"No, but they headed up the valley towards California Gulch."

"How far is that?"

"Oh, 'bout a day's ride," drawled the hostler as he knocked the dottle out of his pipe, stuck the pipe in his pocket and watched Cord as he finished brushing the horse and mule. "You goin' after 'em?"

Cord glanced to the man, nodded, and continued his work.

"They's some bad lookin' characters. The big 'un 'specially, what with that eye patch an' all, but the scrawny one weren't no better. Don't think I'd trust him no more'n I'd trust a rattler! An' both 'em should had oughta swim upriver to get that stink off'n 'em. Better watch yo'sef."

"Tell me 'bout their horses," asked Cord.

"Patch had a black gelding with a white diamond on his forehead and one white sock. The other'n has a bay gelding, with a black spot on his withers, nothin' special 'bout him."

Cord nodded, grabbed his bedroll and asked, "Sleep up there?"

"Ummhmm, two bits fer that, four bits for the animals."

Cord dropped a dollar coin in the man's

outstretched hand, turned to the ladder to the loft and started to climb. He looked over his shoulder and asked, "That café open early?"

"Ummhmm, first light."

———

AFTER A BIG BREAKFAST OF BISCUITS, gravy, steak and eggs, Cord crossed the river to go to the Mercantile store and resupply. He tethered Kwitcher and the mule at the rail, stepped onto the boardwalk and pushed into the store. At the back of the store behind the main counter, he spotted a rack of rifles and on the counter a display of pistols. He was the first customer of the day and the clerk greeted him with, "Mornin' friend. How can I help you?"

"Wanna look at your rifles. Got'ny Spencers?"

"I do," answered the man as he turned his back to Cord and grabbed a Spencer from the rack and lay it on the counter. As he handed the rifle to Cord, he added, "That's got a telescopic sight on it, used by a sniper in the war."

"Let me see that Henry also," added Cord.

"Ain't a Henry, that's the new Winchester Yellow Boy."

"Lemme see it," said Cord, as he examined the Spencer.

As the clerk handed Cord the Winchester, Cord nodded to the rack, "And that Coach Gun also."

"You must be plannin' a war," declared the clerk, looking at Cord with one eyebrow cocked high.

"Nope. I was jumped, shot in the back, robbed and left for dead."

"Goin' after them what done it are you?"

"Somethin' like that," answered Cord, laying the weapons side by side on the counter. "Add a couple boxes of shells for each, and tally it up," instructed Cord.

The clerk used paper and pencil to add the numbers, passed the paper to Cord and Cord dug in his belt for one of the pouches of gold, nodded to the man's gold scales and handed him the pouch. He watched as the clerk poured a small pile of dust in the scale, adjusted the balance and handed the pouch back to Cord.

The clerk stood silent as Cord gathered his weapons and ammunition and walked from the store. He jammed the Spencer in the case that had held the Sharps and the Winchester in the scabbard that had held the Henry, stuffed the ammo in the saddlebags and the remainder in the packs aboard the mule. Tied the coach gun atop the packs and climbed aboard Kwitcher and started north. The sun was still struggling to climb above the mountains in the east, but was doing its best to push long shadows into the valley bottom. The road hugged the west bank of the river, often riding atop the flats that overlooked the waterway, but occasionally dropping into the bottom as well. Cord stopped for his noonin', but only to give the animals a drink and some graze while he lazed in the shade. He heard the rattle of trace chains and the crack of a whip before the stage came into sight, but Cord and his animals were between the road and the river, well out of the way of the stage and the six-up that clattered up the road. The driver had the front of his felt hat pinned back out of his eyes, while his long whiskers were pushed over his shoulders by the wind. He was quite a sight with determined eyes glaring at the road and the rumps of six horses and his limited vocabulary told of his equally limited social life by the names he referred to the horses. A messenger sat atop the stage, his feet on the seat beside the driver and the pair made an odd couple as they rode the Butterfield stage. Luggage and boxes were stacked atop, and the boot showed bulges where more were stuffed under the cover.

The dust cloud settled slowly over the road as the sounds of the passing stage drifted across the valley bottom. Cord chuckled at the brief interlude into his silent retreat, but leaned back against the tree and enjoyed the shade and cool air for a short while longer. The sun stood high overhead when he reined Kwitcher back to the road. The trail of the outlaws had been on the soft shoulder of the road, probably to get a better look at any nearby claims and their trail was easy for Cord to follow.

They had already passed several claims that had been worked and abandoned, and a few that were still being worked. Those that were active had rocker boxes or sluices and usually a cabin or wall tent nearby. None of the prospectors were friendly—all had firearms nearby, but when Cord came to a claim with a recently busted-up sluice and other gear scattered about, he knew something was wrong. Cord reined up, looked a little closer at the workings of the claim that lay on the far side of the river, and spotted what appeared to be a boot showing at the corner of the log cabin.

Cord nudged Kwitcher to the water and they

crossed the gravelly bottomed river that was no deeper than the knees of Kwitcher. As they came from the water, Cord recognized the tracks of the outlaws he was following and dropped his hand to the butt of his pistol that sat in the holster on his left hip. He reined up, looked around and saw no sign of the outlaws, nudged Kwitcher closer to the cabin and a moan from the far side brought Cord to the ground to walk around the cabin, pistol in hand, to find the prospector, bloody and moaning.

Cord went to his side, knelt down, "What happened?" he asked as he looked the man over. He had been shot at least twice, beaten before that, and his face was swollen, black and blue, and bloody.

The man groaned, "Two of 'em, big one, patch on one eye, other'n kinda scrawny, smelly." He struggled with every word and breath, "Took muh gold, four pouches, left me for dead."

"When'd they do it?" asked Cord.

"First light, I was just goin' to muh sluice, they hit me."

Cord looked the man over, saw the bullet wounds, the blood, and looked at the man, "Think we can get you into your cabin?"

The man slowly shook his head, "No, I'm done for," he breathed heavily, looked at Cord, "Just get them two fer me! Tell the sheriff in Oro City."

"What's your name?"

"Shipley, Kirk Shipley," he struggled to pull something from his pocket, "Tell muh wife, Mary, this hyar letter's to her. There's money in the bank for her." He stretched his hand out to Cord, sighed heavily, and fell limp in Cord's arms. Cord jammed the letter into the pocket of his duster, lay the man down and looked around for a shovel. The muscles in his jaw bulged as he gritted his teeth and thought of the outlaws, becoming more resolved than ever to bring justice down on the entire bunch.

11

CALIFORNIA GULCH

DUSK WAS GETTING READY TO DROP ITS CURTAIN ON THE END of day as Cord mounted up and started back upstream beside the Arkansas. He was on the east bank and the main stage road was on the west bank, but he had noticed most of the producing or active claims straddled or rode the banks of tributary creeks that fell from the mountains into the Arkansas River. He also knew that Charlie "One-Eyed" Blunt would not be satisfied nor willing to pass up any other claims. He also thought he had guessed what Blunt would look for in a prospective target: isolated, one-man operation, with easy access and no nearby neighbors. And if he could get ahead of the outlaws, maybe he could be waiting for them at their next target, but to do that, he might have to travel after dark and that would make him a target of every suspicious or cautious claim owner and prospector.

The Shipley claim had been at the mouth of Spring Creek, the many prospectors had taken to naming every gulch and creek for the purpose of marking their recorded claims and handmade signs of every manner marked each of the tributaries. When Cord put Spring Creek behind him, the hills receded and the river coursed through the willow-thick flats, offering easy access to both the river and the mouths of the tributary creeks. Big Union Creek paralleled the river along the willow flats for a short stretch before joining the bigger Arkansas, and was dotted with wall tents and rocker boxes, campfires and vigilant prospectors that usually stood with rifles cradled as they watched Cord ride past. These claims were in the open and close to one another and would not be the kind of targets usually chosen by Blunt and his friend, they would want isolated and solitary.

Cord crossed the Big Union Creek nearer the mouth of the draw that carried the stream and continued on his moonlight ride. The next draw was a dry gulch and the trail pushed around the point of a low-rising finger ridge and faced a long creek that came from higher up and parted a timber-covered butte and a bald-faced butte to make its way across the flats to join the Arkansas. Cord reined up and with the fading light of dusk, he stood in his stirrups and spotted two cook-fires, one near the mouth of the gulch, the other about a quarter-mile upstream. The flickering light of the lower cookfire showed a good-sized wall tent stretched between two lone pines, with two shadowy figures hunkered over the warming flames.

The rattle of trace chains and the crack of a whip caught Cord's attention and he looked across the river to see a stagecoach racing the fading light to make it to its stop somewhere upstream. The stage road crossed the shallows of the river and resumed its pace as the road neared the face of the buttes and turned north to move upstream to its next stop.

After the stage passed and the noise and dust settled, Cord moved closer and called out, "Hello the camp!"

"Who's there!" came an answering bark as both men dropped their tin plates and grabbed for rifles, standing before the fire making silhouettes of themselves.

Cord shook his head at the easy targets they would be, but answered, "I'm friendly! Can I come in?"

"Come ahead, but keep your hands high, if not, the only thing you'll be eatin' is lead!" ordered the same voice that answered before.

Cord nudged Kwitcher forward, bringing the lead line of the mule taut and dragging him behind. With one hand on the reins lifted above the saddle horn, and the other held high above his shoulder, Cord entered the ring of light before the men, reined up and said, "I'm Cordell Beckett, just wanted a place to stop and maybe some coffee."

"Step down, but keep your hands where we can see 'em." The first man, who was the speaker, stepped to the side of the fire, holding his rifle on Cord as he stood before his horse. "What'chu doin' here?" he asked.

"Like I said, lookin' for some coffee and I've got somethin' you need to know. It's about one of your fellow prospectors."

"What is it?" whined the second man, reaching for the coffee pot to pour a cup.

"Mind if I sit down first?" asked Cord, nodding to one of the bigger rocks near the fire.

"Go 'head," answered the first and taller of the two men.

"What's your names?" asked Cord, accepting the offered cup as he seated himself.

"I'm Benjamin Lindsey, and this is Henry or Hank Modine. Now what's this we need to know?"

"Well," began Cord, and related the story about Kirk Shipley and his claim and what the outlaws did. When Cord described the two outlaws, the men before him looked at one another and back to Cord, wide-eyed. Cord noticed the reaction and asked, "What?"

"We saw a couple like that just 'fore dark. They was o'er yonder at the crossin' and they climbed that little hump and was lookin' all around with binoculars. I saw 'em cuz I was lookin' at them with our telescope. But they din't do nuthin'. They just left."

"Where'd they go?"

"Dunno, I was watchin', turned to Ben and looked back an' they was gone."

Cord dropped his hand to rub Blue behind the ears, finished his coffee and looked to the two men. "Yours is the kind of claim these two seem to like to hit. Isolated, but of course, there's two of you and they usually hit solitary targets, but..." he shrugged. He looked back up at them. "They usually hit first thing in the mornin', from what I can tell, so if it's alright with you fellas, I'll camp back up the creek a ways, but I'll be down here, hidin' out, at first light, so if they come, I might get a shot at 'em."

"You mean you'd just shoot 'em?" asked Hank, a little surprised at their new acquaintance. "Ain't that kinda like murder?"

Cord shook his head, "After what they done, you can call it murder if you want, it's just that I'd rather they were killed before they murder me or someone else. But don't worry, I'll give 'em a chance." But as he shook his head, he was thinking about the chance he would give would be a mighty small chance if any. These were not the kind of men to take chances with, not at all.

Cord stood, looked at the two men and turned back to his horse. He swung aboard and with a nod to the men, rode from the campfire light toward the end of the butte that lay behind them. As he neared the point of the butte, the sun dropped below the mountains in the west and cast long shadows across the flats, offering little light for Cord to turn back into the brush heavy draw and find a good spot to make his camp.

He tethered Kwitcher and the mule within reach of the water that chuckled down the draw, working its way through the scrub oak brush and the willows and more. A slight clearing with deep grass offered ample cover for Cord to roll out his blankets under the alder and cottonwood.

It was a restless night for Cord, often tossing and turning in his blankets, staring at the moon that was waxing full, and remembering Bird and their times together. Although his wound was healing, it still was uncomfortable at best and sometimes a stabbing pain would make him wince unexpectedly. He rolled to his left side, looked at Blue lying nearby and Kwitcher and the mule standing hipshot at the edge of the trees, but there was nothing disturbing, just the usual night sounds of the nearby chuckling creek, the chirp of the nighthawk, and the distant howl of a coyote whose cry went unanswered. He was restless and tried to pray, but prayer did not come easy. He was still trying to understand why it seemed that every time he drew close to someone, they were taken from him. He shook his head, rolled over, cringed at the pain and moved to his back.

He had dozed off, but the stirring of Blue brought Cord instantly awake. The early morning sky was a dusty blue/grey as he crawled from his bedroll, and grabbed up his Winchester, checked the load, and with a handful of bullets in his duster pocket, he jammed his hat on his head and started through the brush to make his way back to the camp of the prospectors. As he neared the wall tent, he dropped behind a thicket of alder, peering through the branches to the claim site, but nothing moved. He heard the snort and snore from the wall tent and knew the two prospectors were still in their bunks.

Without showing himself, Cord moved to where he had a better view of the claim and the nearby area, and choosing a pair of alder bushes, he sat down, facing the claim, but still in the deep shadows of the brush. He did not have to wait long until he heard the clatter of hooves on the rocky trail as two riders neared the camp. They rode into the clearing, both with rifles over the pommels of their saddles and they stopped before the wall tent.

The big man, Blunt, called out in a gruff voice, "You in the tent! Show yousef'!" and jacked a round into his rifle so the sound would be heard by the prospectors.

Their backs were to Cord and no more than fifteen

yards away as Cord stepped into the open and jacked a round into the Yellow Boy Winchester. The rattle of the hardware racketed through the quiet and caused the two outlaws to sit up tall in their saddles as Cord said in a calm, almost quiet voice, "And you two, throw those rifles on the ground!" It was a commanding voice that broke the stillness and the big man started to turn in his saddle, but Cord dropped the hammer, and his bullet busted the stock of the rifle in Blunt's hands causing the man to shout, "Wha!!" and start to turn.

"Don't move!" ordered Cord, glancing from the big man to the scrawny one.

The two prospectors flipped the flap of their tent back and stepped out, rifles in hand, and looked at their visitors. Cord called, "Cover 'em, I'm comin' over!" and stepped from the brush.

"Where's your camp?" growled Cord, moving to face the two outlaws.

When he showed himself, the big man looked at Cord, "You!"

"Ummhmm, me. Next time you sneak up behind someone to shoot 'em in the back, you might want to make sure they're dead. But wait, you won't be doin' that will you?" chuckled Cord, "because I might just hang you right here! Or over there where there's a taller tree," nodded Cord.

The big man turned to look at the tree, using his move to mask his grabbing for his pistol, but Cord saw what he was doing and before Blunt could bring the pistol to bear, Cord fired two quick rounds from the Winchester, both bullets taking the man in the chest and driving him from his saddle to fall to the ground in

a heap. Cord stepped around to look at the downed
man, saw blood coming from his mouth and his eyes
wide with fear. He struggled for breath, tried to talk,
but foam and blood came from his mouth as his last
breath was exhaled and he slumped in death, his big
body rolling to his face.

The big man's horse had spooked and jumped
backward away from the body when the big man left
the saddle, and Hank had grabbed the reins to settle
him down while Ben kept his rifle on the scrawny one.
Cord stepped beside Ben, looked up at the scrawny one
and ordered him to the ground and the man slid to the
ground, keeping his hands high and his eyes wide with
fear.

Cord looked at him, "What's your name anyway?"

"Uh, uh, I'm Judd Pollack. Why?"

"Wanna know what to put on your grave marker,"
answered a sober Cord. "But before we do that, where
were you and Blunt there gonna meet the others?"

"Uh, uh, what others?"

"You know what others. The rest of the bunch he
rode with out here from back east. He rode with a
bunch of Red Legs, but I don't think you were one
of 'em."

"No, no, I weren't one. Uh, uh, he did say he was
gonna meet some friens in a day or so, but I dunno
where," whimpered Judd, "Don' kill me, pleeeeze."

Cord turned to look at Ben, "Is there any law
around here?"

Ben shook his head, "Just miner's court, thas all."

Cord nodded, looked at Judd, "Here's what we'll do.
You take us to where you have the rest of your gold
stashed, you know, that you took off the others back

down the trail, and we'll turn you over to miner's court. Or...we can just hang you right'chere."

"No, no! I'll take you, really I will!" declared the scrawny Judd, his knees shaking so hard he wet himself.

12

COURT

Word spread quickly and by high noon, many of the miners were gathered just outside Oro City near the diggings of the man chosen to lead the Miner's Court. A big man sat on an oversized three-legged stool beside a massive pink granite boulder. He dropped a twelve-pound sledge on the boulder and growled, "Court will come t'order!" He handled the sledge like most men would wield a carpenter's hammer and the growl of his voice echoed the image of the man who almost dwarfed his two-ton granite desk.

"Bucky" Braham stood two hands over six feet and if there was a big enough scale to weigh him it would show somewhere in the neighborhood of three hundred pounds, and very little of it was around his waist. Broad shoulders and massive upper arms forced him to turn to the side to fit through the normal sized door and it was said he had little use for black powder in his mine for he was able the drive drill steel one handed and would split the normal rock formation with his drill.

"Who's bringin' the charges?" growled Bucky, looking around the restless crowd.

"We are!" declared Ben and Hank together as they stood and looked around.

"What'chu got to say?"

Ben began the testimony with the account of earlier in the day at their claim, including when Cord joined them and warned them. Ben finished with, "And Cord there shot the big fella right outta his saddle, one shot done it!" he declared, nodding his head and looking from his partner to the judge.

"Where's this Cordell Beckett?" asked Judge Bucky.

Cord stood, lifted a hand, "Right here, Judge."

The judge motioned him forward and asked, "Why'd you shoot that man?"

"Keep him from shooting me," answered a sober Cord. The response drawing chuckles, laughter, and nodding heads that agreed with his deed.

The judge nodded, "What made you think he was gonna shoot you?"

Cord shook his head, "Probably when he was grabbing his pistol when he turned. We already made 'em drop their rifles. He also killed another prospector a little ways downriver, fella by the name of Kirk Shipley," Cord paused as the name drew a reaction from the crowd. He continued with, "Kirk lived long enough to identify the two that we encountered this mornin' and because of that, I was not in a trusting mood."

"You a lawman or sumpin'?" asked the judge.

"No, just a man looking for justice, from him and the others like him."

"What'chu mean others?"

"His partner was a part of a bunch of Red Legs I

followed out here from Missouri. Already found a few of 'em"—he nodded to Judd Pollack—"his partner was one of 'em, and we were tryin' to get more information out of him about the others, but so far, he ain't said much."

The judge growled, looked from Cord to Pollack, and asked, "That right? You an' yore partner kilt Kirk Shipley, stole his poke?"

"Uh, uh, uh," stammered the scrawny scared outlaw, glancing from Cord to the judge, "Uh, yeah, I guess so."

"You *guess* so?" roared the judge, glaring at the wiry figure, "Either you did or didn't, which is it?"

"Blunt did it! He did! I din't shoot nobody!" whined Pollack, looking around at the angry visages that made up the court.

"But you was with him?"

"Yeah, I reckon."

"And the two of you was gonna rob an' kill at that claim this mornin'?" snarled Bucky.

Pollack just nodded, trying to duck his head and neck into his shoulders to hide from the wrath of the judge. He glanced from Cord to the judge and back, pleading for mercy with his looks and whimpers, but mercy was not forthcoming.

"All in favor of guilty say 'Aye'!" stated the judge. The crowd roared with an *Aye* that rolled across the flats for everyone to hear.

The judge nodded, lifted his gavel and dropped it, making everyone flinch thinking the granite boulder would split, but as the sledge dropped, the judge pronounced, "Guilty! Hang him!" The crowd surged forward, but Cord stepped in front of the man, "Tell me where you were gonna meet the others!"

The man whimpered, "Porcupine Gulch, they got a camp up there!"

Cord was pushed aside, and the crowd grabbed the man, dragging him along toward a big cottonwood near the creek and Cord stepped away. He watched as the crowd stampeded toward the creek, knowing the anger of the prospectors at one of the many outlaws that would steal from the hard-working men. They seldom had the chance for retribution and all their frustration and anger came to the surface as they struck out against this one man that was within their reach and justice. When he and the two prospectors had taken Pollack to their camp, they found the pouches of gold taken from Shipley, but Cord's Sharps, Henry, and coach gun were not among the belongings. When Pollack was asked, he pleaded ignorance and their patience had worn thin, resulting in the hurry-up jaunt to miner's court.

Cord looked at the big man that had served as judge and had remained seated as the crowd scampered away to mete out their justice. Cord stepped closer to ask, "Porcupine Gulch, whereabouts will I find it?"

Bucky Braham grunted, "Don'know why you'd wanna go up there. Ain't no gold there, but there are a few claims, abandoned most of 'em, none of 'em showed color."

With a nod of his head, Cord motioned to the crowd, "He said the rest of their bunch has a camp up there."

Bucky frowned, looking at Cord, and grunted, "Foller the river," pointing to the lower reaches of California Gulch, "north. It'll be 'bout five, six mile, near the north end of a wide park, they call it Tennessee Park for the cricks that run into it. Porcupine's a little crick comes from the west. Those hills are thick with timber, but Porcupine cuts through 'em, you'll recognize it cuz o' some beaver ponds an' such. The crick ain't more a couple feet wide, ankle deep, hardly 'nuff fer pannin'. Never heard o' nobody gettin' color up thar."

Cord nodded and started to turn away until Bucky added, "If'n yore goin' up thataway after more like that'n, you might do better if'n you looked more like a prospector 'steada bounty hunter. You know, get'chu some pans an' shovels, hobnail boots 'stead o' them mocassins, that way they won't be suspicious of you an' might even come to you 'steada you huntin' them."

Cord nodded, "Thanks, might be a good idea. Where's the nearest miners' supply post?"

Bucky pointed toward Oro City upstream on California Gulch, "Thataway."

———

MINER'S MERCANTILE was a sod-roofed log building with a door and one window facing the hitch rail where Cord tied off Kwitcher and the mule. He pushed open the door, paused before entering the darker interior, but a voice hailed him, "C'mon in an' welcome!"

Cord pushed into the shadowy interior, saw a man with a leather apron standing behind a plank counter and puffing on a corn cob pipe. "What can I do ya' fer?" asked the man.

Cord frowned, looked about, "Need some supplies.

Couple pans, shovels, a pick, some coffee, and four boxes .44 cartridges."

He looked at the man who started to turn, but when Cord said cartridges, the clerk turned back to frown at Cord, "You gonna pan for it or shoot it?"

Cord frowned as the man clarified, "The gold man, the gold," he chuckled at his own humor and began gathering the requested gear. As he stacked things on the counter, he looked at Cord, "Ever panned for gold before?"

"Nope."

"So, you don't know what yore doin', eh?"

Cord chuckled, "Nope."

The clerk looked around, leaning to the side to look out the open door and window. He picked up one of the pans, "Foller me," motioning to Cord as he walked to the door. He spoke over his shoulder, "Got me a water trough out'chere an' I'll show you a thing or two."

He stepped to the trough, pan in hand, then bent to grab a handful of dirt, looked at Cord, and began, "Now, here's what'chu do. The soil's in the pan, so you scoop up some water, swirl it around and wash the soil, and be careful, but let the heavy stuff drop to the bottom, then tip it like this..." and he continued for two or three tries, just to demonstrate. He finished when he said, "And as you see, we din't get no gold. But if there's gold, when you wash the dirt, it'll settle to the bottom cuz it's heavier. Then slowly pour out the water, scoop up the gold an' put it in your pouch, and do it all over again."

"Sounds easy enough," responded Cord as he followed the clerk back into the store.

The clerk continued, "Now, you might need a

hammer, maybe some nails, cuz you'll prob'ly wanna build a rocker box or a sluice..."

Cord could see the clerk was calculating all he could sell to this greenhorn he thought Cord to be, but Cord said, "If I get any color, I'll come back for that. For now, this is all I need."

He paid for the goods, put them on his packs, tying them atop everything else so they would be conspicuous and stepped aboard Kwitcher. The clerk had followed him out of the store, and Cord asked, "There a eatin' place near? Maybe a saloon? And a livery or a place to sleep?"

The clerk chuckled, "You'll find all that in Oro City. Used to be more, but when things started dryin' up, most folks left for richer places."

Cord spent some more time with the chatty clerk, picking his brain about prospecting, equipment, and more, until he thought he knew enough to at least look the part. He was not concerned about finding gold, although he would keep any he found, but he was more concerned about the outlaw renegades that had once been Red Legs. His suspicion was that they were in this area to enrich themselves at the expense and labor of others, but he wanted to put a stop to their thievery. He mounted up and started toward the livery and to find a place to eat and perhaps get a little more information about the outlaws.

13

PORCUPINE

"Less'n you wanna go into town, the only place you'll get sumpin' to eat is at the Lucky Lady. It's a saloon mostly, but they got a kitchen an' she cooks ever now'n then. But be careful, cuz she ain't lucky an' she ain't no lady!" declared the smithy at the livery that lay just west of the rest of the business buildings, such as they were. The town had seen better days and at one time had several thousand more inhabitants, but when the color began to fade, those searching for instant riches left. What had been mostly placer mining and profitable, would become the work of machines with hydraulic mining and dredging, but now most claims were marked by broken rockers, sluices, and other debris.

Cord left the livery and walked across the road to the Lucky Lady. It was his practice to try to be as inconspicuous as possible and he stepped to the end of the bar, nodded to barkeep when he offered, "Beer?"

As the man sat the mug before him, Cord asked, "You have anything to eat?"

"Yup, she's cooked up some bear steaks with taters, bread n' gravy. Four bits."

"I'll have a plate, o'er to that table," motioned Cord to a table that stood against the far wall and out of the way in the shadowy corner.

The bartender nodded and turned to the kitchen as Cord carried his mug of beer to the table. He sat with the corner walls behind him and facing the door. He doffed his hat, hung it on the nearby chair, and slipped off his duster, hanging it on the chair back. He sat down, leaned forward, elbows on the table and looked about the room. There were several tables, but only two were occupied, one with two men, the other with four. Two men stood at the bar, talking quietly to one another. The conversation of the four men could be easily heard and Cord never looked at the men, glancing about the room and down to the floor, but listened carefully.

A portly woman, a little past middle-aged, with greying hair and ruffled attire, waddled toward him, carrying a plate and a coffee pot with a cup dangling. She asked, "You the one what wants to eat?"

"That's right," answered Cord, frowning at the untidy woman as she sat down the plate, pushed the hair away from her face and sat down the cup, poured the coffee, splashing a little onto the table. She started to turn when Cord asked, "You the Lucky Lady?"

"That's right, what of it?" she snarled, holding the coffee pot in a threatening manner as if she was ready to douse Cord with the steaming hot brew.

"Just curious, ma'am, that's all."

"Hmmmph," she grumbled as she turned and marched to the kitchen.

"You're lucky you din't get the whole pot in yore lap, stranger!" came a voice from the table with four men.

Cord looked at the group, grinned, "I thought I was about to!" he chuckled and turned to his plate.

The men continued to lift their drinks and talk among themselves, but Cord was able to listen as he ate, never looking at the men, but always appearing to be in his own little realm.

"Yeah, ol' Jackson said there was mebbe ten, twelve of 'em an' none of 'em had any prospectin' gear at'all. Sounds to me they're up to no good," said the same man that spoke to Cord. He was sitting with his back to Cord as he faced the others.

"Sure sounds like it, but what you reckon they be up to?" asked another.

"If they ain't minin', and they ain't settlin', and they ain't got no livestock, just what else is there?"

"I'm thinkin' just like that fella we hung, prob'ly lookin' to jump claims!"

"Nah, jumpin' claims mean they'd be wantin' the claims and that comes with work. I'd lay money on them just doin' like that fella did, robbin' the prospectors. What'chu think they'd get if they hit all the claims down the line, say at least one pouch of twenty, thirty ounces at each claim, an' there's what, at least a hunnert claims. That'd be two to three thousand ounces at $27 that'd be o'er $80,000!"

The men fell silent, looking at one another, and without another word, they finished their drinks, pushed back their chairs and headed for the door, undoubtedly headed back to their claims.

———

CORD PUT Oro City and California Gulch behind him and
started north on the stage road, although this road
showed less use than that south of the gulch. What
would usually be considered as the headwaters of the
Arkansas River was called Tennessee Creek by the
locals. The wetlands of the creek with beaver dams and
thickets of willow and berry bushes, was often pushed
aside for gold claims, some that were working, others
abandoned, as the winding creek twisted its way south.
The stage road hugged the east bank of the creek and
bent to the northeast as the valley opened to what
locals called Tennessee Park, probably named after an
early trapper or prospector that hailed from Tennessee.

Cord crossed the creek as the sun climbed over the
snow-capped eastern mountains, painting the snow-
covered peaks a brilliant reddish orange as it bent its
rays into the valley and chased the shadows into
hiding. The creek made a wide bend to the west as it
worked its way through the flats of the park, pushing
the thickets of willows, alders, and berry bushes closer
to the tree line that showed as a thick carpet of green
that lay on the foothills of the west slope. Cord watched
for the cuts through the timber that would carry the
feeder creeks, looking for the one that twisted its way
through beaver dams and cut its way from the higher
mountains by separating the tall pines to make its way
below.

It was a little more than a mile, by Cord's guessti-
mate, when he spotted the cut in the trees and the
slight dip in the hills that showed the presence of a
creek. He nudged Kwitcher toward the feeder creek that
he guessed to be Porcupine and stopped at creek's edge,
stood in his stirrups and looked about, searching for

recent tracks of riders going into the thicker timber, and for a likely looking spot for a claim to set up his camp.

The mouth of the gulch was about four hundred yards wide, narrowing quickly as it came from the timber. The little feeder creek, probably called Porcupine Creek, twisted its way between beaver dams and from the nearest dam to the bigger Tennessee Creek was a good hundred yards. Cord nodded to himself, and decided on setting up his claim at the mouth of Porcupine Creek. He set about his work immediately, picketing Kwitcher in the willows, within reach of both graze and water. He dropped the packs from the mule, taking an axe, a whipsaw, and rope, he headed for the timber.

By noon, he had felled several trees, dragged them to his claim, and begun using the one-man crosscut whipsaw to make him some lumber for a rocker box and maybe a sluice. He wanted his claim to have all the makings of a real claim and busied himself in the doing of it.

It was late afternoon when he sat back to look at the frame for his rocker box with a touch of pride. He sat on one of the logs, doffed his hat and wiped his brow, and the uplifted head of the mule caught his attention as the mule stood still, looking toward the gulch at three riders that came from the trees. Cord had kept his rifle within reach, and the shotgun hidden, but close. His pistol sat on his hip, but his loose hanging vest covered the butt. He replaced his hat, stayed seated, crossed his arms over his chest and watched as the riders came near.

It was easy to spot the leader of the pack, for there

is always one that sees himself as bigger, meaner, tougher, than the others and usually pushes himself to the front. That man sat tall in his saddle, wore a leather vest over a linen shirt, and canvas britches tucked into his boot tops. Red hair protruded from under his floppy felt hat and reddish whiskers dotted his face. He reined up, leaned on the pommel of his saddle and pushed his hat back on his head as he grinned at Cord.

"Where'd you come from?" he asked.

"Who's askin'?" replied Cord.

"I'm Red Clark, who're you?"

"I'm Cordell Beckett."

"Like I said, where'd you come from?"

Cord nodded to the cut between the buttes that carried Tennessee Creek into the Arkansas without answering.

"Where you goin'?" added Red, sitting up and dropping his hand to his side near his pistol.

Cord pointed between his feet, "I'm here."

Red shook his head, "Uhnuhn, no you ain't. You're leavin' right now, or we'll be buryin' you!" as he dropped his hand to his pistol and started to draw.

Cord snatched his pistol from the holster, brought it to bear on the leader and dropped the hammer before Red leveled his pistol. The roar of gunfire echoed across the flat, the horses jerked at the startling blast, and the others jerked on the reins to control their mounts. Red slid from his saddle, dropping in a heap in the deep grass as Cord dove behind the log, grabbing his coach gun as he hit the ground.

One of the others had grabbed at his pistol but when he fired the shot went wild as his horse jerked, but a blast of double ought buck roared from under the log driving the man from his saddle into a bloody mess in the grass. The third man had struggled to control his horse, grabbed his pistol and fired at the log, splitting the bark as he fired repeatedly, but Cord had rolled away, grabbing his Winchester as he did. He came up about eight feet away and levered a round into the chamber, just as the third man swung his pistol for a shot, but the hammer fell on an empty chamber, the usual empty chamber most men kept for safety as they rode with pistols in holsters.

He looked down at the empty pistol, up at Cord, and Cord barked, "Drop it!"

The man dropped his empty pistol, lifted both hands and whimpered, "Don't shoot, don't shoot."

"Get down," ordered Cord and watched as the man awkwardly stepped to the ground, trying to keep his hands raised so he wouldn't be shot. He had stepped down on the far side of the horse, ducked under the horse's neck and stood on the right side of his horse, looking wide-eyed at Cord. Cord asked, "What's your name?"

"Bill Coogan," he whimpered.

"What was his name?" asked Cord, motioning to the second man that was killed.

"That was Bill Hendricks."

Cord nodded, recognizing the name from his list of Red Legs. "How long you been ridin' with the Red Legs?"

The man frowned, looking at Cord, "Uh, I weren't no Red Leg, but how'd you know *they* was Red Legs?"

"Been followin' 'em all the way from Kansas. How many left up there?" nodding to the gulch that carried Porcupine Creek.

"Uh, with us," nodding to the downed men and referring to himself, "there was eight, but there was three others that we was waitin' on."

"They ain't comin'," declared Cord. "You say you weren't one of 'em, Red Legs, I mean?"

"No, no, I din't join up till they come into this country. I weren't no good at prospectin' an' I needed some money, so..." he shrugged.

"Then I don't want you. If I let you go, will you leave the country, not meet up with that bunch? You know, straighten out your life and quit outlawin'?"

"Yeah, yeah, I promise!" declared the man, his nervousness showing as his knees shook and he was dancing as if he was needing to find an outhouse.

"Then git!" ordered Cord.

14

PROSPECTING

BILL COOGAN RODE AWAY WITH THE TWO HORSES OF THE outlaws in tow. That left Cord to dispose of the bodies, but that was no problem in a place where fresh diggings were expected and Cord made short work of two shallow graves well away from the water, preferring not to have his water polluted by the likes of those two. When he finished the graves, covering them over with fresh dirt but scattering some of the dry topsoil about so the digging would not be too conspicuous, he set about making his claim look the part. He hastily finished putting together his rocker box, did some random digging near the stream and away from it, lay his tools about, leaning the pick against one of the remaining logs and the axe buried in the log.

He sat down to take a break and look around and decided he needed to lay out his bedroll and put together a cookfire with coffee pot and more. He wanted to make everything look like he was here to stay, at least for a little while and like most prospectors, not too permanent with the need to find color or move on. He sat down to await the perking of the coffee and withdrew his list from his shirt pocket. He unfolded the now worn paper and looked at the names. He had crossed off Duncan Pitts, the drunk that was lazing around the fort or rather the so-called town outside the fort where the soldiers would spend their money on watered down booze and worn-out women. Although Pitts was still alive, or was when he last saw him, his name was crossed off the list he had compiled when he first learned the names of the gang of Red Legs from one of their own, Bill Tough, outside of Leavenworth. Bill had established a good reputation as the owner and operator of a livery stable, and was doing his best to live down his past. Cord had been impressed with the man and had already learned he had not been a part of the rapine and murder that went on after the war. Now his visit with Bill Tough seemed like an eternity past, but the presence of the former Red Legs had brought the past into the present. He read the names of the others that were lined out, *Charles "Doc"Jennison, Red Clark, Jim Lane, Charles "One-Eyed" Blunt.* And the names that remained, *Newt Morrison, Jack Hays, James Flood, and Jerry Malcolm.*

Bill Coogan had said there were five men left, and Cord had four names on his list. But he would be at a dangerous disadvantage if he tried to take the four at once, and there could always be more, what with their penchant of recruiting others that were bent on the outlaw life. That seemed like it would be a good way or a foolish way to die, and he was not real anxious to meet his Maker quite yet. He needed to know more about the men and how they worked. He wanted to see their camp, get a better idea about the men, their habits, their plans and more, but how? His reverie was interrupted by the sound of horses coming from the edge of the trees further up Porcupine Creek, he heard the clatter of hooves as several horses crossed the shallow creek and came into sight from the shadows of the black timber.

It was evident by their appearance, dress, and manner, they were not prospectors. Their attire was that of horsemen or former cavalry. Although less than a hundred yards away, it was evident they bristled with weapons. Each man carried at least two pistols, scabbards with rifles hung beneath the fender skirts of their saddles, and although they were well out into the flat away from the creek and Cord's prospect sight, furtive glances from every man were evident.

Cord did his best to show little attention to the men, trying to appear busy with his diggings, driving his shovel into the gravelly bank, adding to the pile to be placed into his rocker box. He paused, stood tall, doffed his hat and wiped his brow, and returned to his busy work. The riders paid little attention, but Cord knew he had been seen and talked about. He grinned to himself, shook his head slightly, and as they rode into the cut that carried Porcupine Creek and Tennessee Creek through the timber and to its confluence with the Arkansas, he lifted his hand, formed a pistol with his fingers and dropped the hammer of his thumb as they rode from sight.

Cord stuck the shovel in the dirt and walked into the willows to saddle up Kwitcher. As he worked, he thought about the outlaws, knowing it would take a while for them to do whatever they were up to in town, and he should have enough time to scout their camp, and begin to formulate a plan on his next action against the men.

He swung aboard Kwitcher, motioned Blue to take to the trail and started backtracking the riders that came from the trees. But Cord was surprised as the terrain was misleading. What had appeared to him as the Porcupine Gulch that showed narrow clearings that pointed to the higher mountains through what appeared to be a long valley, was a waterless cut that led nowhere. A short distance inside the black timber, the creek made a dog-leg bend around the point of a timbered ridge, and cut a narrow gulch through the low timber-covered buttes that meandered around the hill-tops, and after over a half-mile, opened into a long narrow valley thick with willows and a few beaver ponds. Then the creek bent back to the south and west before opening into a long clearing that stretched about a quarter-mile toward the high mountains, and lay about two hundred yards wide.

Cord reined up, stood in his stirrups for a better look around, sniffed the air and smelled stale smoke from a cookfire. He was cautious, not knowing if there were any other members of the outlaw gang that might have remained in camp. He watched Blue, but the dog was only interested in a rabbit that cut away from under some nearby willows and the rambunctious dog eagerly gave chase. Cord shook his head as he grinned at his canine friend, and nudged Kwitcher forward. He stayed close to the tree line, working his way along the edge of the park, but when the trees lay back to the south, he was exposed but in the shade of the late afternoon long shadows. He paused, looking about, and pushed forward.

As he neared what he guessed to be the campsite, he called out, "Hello the camp! I'm friendly an' comin' in!"

There was no response, but Cord rode slowly toward the opening in the trees that showed what appeared to be another smaller clearing beyond the narrow opening. No answer came to his call and he moved forward, his right hand resting on the butt of his pistol, but the clearing held no camp, just a little bog with cattails and willows. Cord chuckled at himself, reined Kwitcher around and moved back into the larger clearing. Keeping to the tree line and the shadows, he came to another break, saw the tracks of many horses and backtracked them into the smaller clearing and the campsite.

It was evident they had been here for some time, with bedrolls still scattered about, two cookfires that smoldered, other trash and more scattered about. Part of a deer carcass hung from a high branch, showing sign of having most of the meat cut away. But there was nothing that showed any special preparations or precautions made for their defense. Cord thought that to be common for those that thought themselves smarter and tougher than any others, believing that no one would dare come after them for fear of the consequences. Cord looked down at Blue as he sniffed about the gear, chuckled, "Guess we might just hafta surprise 'em, huh Blue?"

The dog lifted his head, cocked it to the side as he looked at Cord, and wagged his tail as if agreeing with whatever Cord said.

Cord ground-tied Kwitcher, and started a walk about the camp, then into the trees that surrounded the clearing, looking at the terrain, the view from different points on the hillside that loomed high above the clearing, and looked for any game trails that would offer access. As he surveyed the area, he leaned low, twisting and turning about and looking through the timber for the possible access to the clearing. He grinned as he saw daylight to the south of the camp, went back to Kwitcher and stepped aboard. He motioned to Blue, and they left the camp, being certain to use only the trail used by their horses to leave no unusual sign.

He went back to the bigger clearing with the bog, stayed near the trees and pushed through the trees, following a faint game trail that took him over a low saddle and into the valley beyond. Taking that valley to the east, it soon dropped him into the park that held the Tennessee Creek and his own prospect camp. He grinned and nudged Kwitcher through the trees and headed back to his camp as he began to formulate a plan. As he rode, he remembered the words of his father that echoed his time in the war, *"Offense is better than defense. If you can be on the attack, you are in control of the fight, but defending, you're depending on what the enemy will do, and that gives him the tactical advantage. When you take the initiative, you usually determine the outcome."* His father fought with the British during the Battle of Pinjarra and had received an officer's commission. He also fought with the Ottoman Empire as an officer during the revolt in Tripolitania, but refused to talk about his experience or exploits, but often passed on the wisdom gained by his experience.

He looked at Blue who trotted alongside, watching every move, and asked, "Well boy, what're we gonna do now?"

15

PLAN

CORD WAS STOPPED BY THE WIDE PARK THAT BRISTLED WITH currant, serviceberry, and buffalo berry bushes that were intermingled with willow and sage. But it was the movement beyond the brushy flats that gave Cord pause, making him rein up beside the trees and in the deep shadows of late afternoon. It was about a half-mile to Porcupine Creek and the site of his camp, but several riders were there. Cord reached back and grabbed his binoculars from the saddlebags, lifted them for a quick look, and he counted six men, three had dismounted and two of those were rifling through his scattered equipment and gear. The mule had been tethered further back into the thicker willows and had not been discovered, but Cord was not willing to bet the pack animal would remain still and unseen. One of the men was down on one knee, looking at the dirt and undoubtedly examining the tracks of those that had visited his camp and probably the tracks left by Cord when he rode out and backtracked the outlaws.

His temptation was to unlimber the Winchester

and ride in with rifle blazing, but with six men, it would be risky at best, foolish at worst. He might luckily drop two, maybe three, but the others would easily outgun him. This was one of those times that his father's words to *take the initiative* would be best ignored, unless he was to take the initiative and disappear into the trees. Cord took another lingering look at the outlaws, glanced to the trees, and nudged Kwitcher into the woods. He motioned Blue alongside, and explained to himself and the dog, "We'll keep outta sight, maybe get closer for a better look, but you stay close now, y'hear?"

He reined up within the black timber, stepped down and tethered Kwitcher. With the Winchester in hand and Blue at his side, Cord stealthily worked his way to the edge of the trees, always staying under cover and in the shadows. He dropped to one knee behind a big ponderosa and leaned around for a closer look with his binoculars. The group was at the edge of Porcupine Creek, the two men that had scattered his gear were coming across the creek to join the others. The man on the ground was motioning to the tracks, talking to the man who was apparently the leader, and both looking up the trail to the trees, the same trail followed by Cord when he searched out their camp. As the two men crossed the creek, Cord recognized one as the same man who called himself Bill Coogan and pleaded for mercy, convincing Cord to let him go and take the horses of the two men he killed. Cord shook his head, remembering the man had promised to leave the country and never come back. So much for the promise of outlaws.

The temptation was to cut loose with his rifle and

take a toll of the murderers of his family, but he fought with himself and watched as the rest mounted up and the group started up the trail with the tracker leading the way and often leaning down to look at the tracks. Cord knew they were looking at the single set of tracks going upstream, his tracks, and the tracks of Kwitcher were obviously different from the others of the outlaws. But if they were able to find his trail about their camp and leaving their camp, they might continue to follow his sign through the trees and around the butte to his current location.

As soon as the band disappeared into the trees, Cord returned to Kwitcher, mounted up and went to his camp to gather his gear together. He knew they had wrecked most of his handiwork, but he needed to get whatever remained, especially his pack mule. He crossed the creek, pushed into the thicker willows where the mule was tethered, and stepped down. He began gathering his gear, putting it into the panniers and parfleche. The coffee pot had been kicked about but appeared to be usable, the cups had been stomped, and the shovel had the handle broken. The axe and pick had been tossed into the brush along the creek, but were undamaged. He was coming from the willows, pick and axe in hand, when he heard the clatter of hooves and turned to see two riders coming from the trees, they were two of the six seen earlier and they were coming with broad and evil grins.

They reined to a stop on the far creek bank, both leaning forward on their pommels and as they looked at Cord, one spoke, "So, Jim, whatchu think we oughta do? Shoot him or take him back to the boys?"

The second man chuckled, twisting in his seat as if

he had bugs in his britches, and cackled, "Cain't we do both, Jack?"

They were across the little creek, but no more than a dozen feet away and Cord turned away as if looking into the bushes, dropped the shovel to one side to distract the two, but brought the pick around and with a powerful swing from his shoulder, he sent the pick tumbling end over end toward the one called Jack. Wide eyes showed sudden fear, an open mouth started to scream, but the tumbling pick buried its narrow metal head deep in the man's upper chest at the base of his throat. The impact drove the man back and he jerked on the reins of his mount, trying to scream as nothing but blood came from his mouth. He slumped over and slid from his saddle to fall in a heap on his back on the grassy bank.

The second man was so startled, he froze in place, watching the horrific sight of his friend being killed by a thrown pickaxe. He struggled to control his mount, turned with wide eyes to look at Cord who was looking at him over the sights of his Colt and growled, "Well, what'chu gonna do Jim?"

"Uh, uh, uh...." stammered Jim, gripping the reins with white knuckles and staring at Cord with fright-filled eyes, afraid to move.

"Then step down, Jim. I can't have you runnin' off to your friends, now, can I?"

"Uh, uh, uh...." he stammered, slowly lifting his free hand high and starting to step down. When he stood beside his mount, Cord motioned him to cross the creek, and the frightened man waded the little creek and stood before Cord, both hands held high. Cord stepped behind him, lifted the pistol from the man's holster, slipped the big knife from the scabbard on the opposite hip, and tossed both into the brush.

"Now, belly down in the grass there, Jim," ordered Cord. As the man bent down, went to hands and knees and reluctantly to his belly, Cord added, "Hands behind your back, Jim."

The man obliged, and Cord tied his hands together, took a loop around his feet and drew them up to his hands and tied them off. Cord pulled the neckerchief from the man's neck and blindfolded him with it, and stepped back.

"Now Jim, I'm gonna leave you like that, and if you're lucky, your friends will find you before the mountain lions or grizzly bears that prowl around here, or maybe even that pack of wolves I heard last night. Now, what you're gonna do is tell your boss, Newt is it? Anyway, tell him and the others they best leave the country 'fore I find 'em. You've already lost six of your men. Let me see..." as he pulled his list out of his pocket, "Bill Tough, Duncan Pitts, 'Doc' Jennison, Red Clark, Jim Lane, Charles 'One-Eyed' Blunt, Dave Poole, and now this'n," nodding to the dead man with the pickaxe in his chest, "I reckon that's Jack Hayes." As he spoke he crossed off the name of Jack Hays. "So, that's eight of your men gone. So, counting you and that latest addition, Bill Coogan, you've only got five left, of course that includes the new recruit. So, it might be best for your bunch to high-tail it outta these mountains 'fore I come lookin' for the rest of you."

Cord had been loading his gear while he talked, and now swung aboard Kwitcher, grabbed the lead line of his pack mule and with a last look at his pickaxe that he chose to leave in the chest of Jack Hayes, he

said, "See ya!" and rode from the flats. He had disappeared into the black timber on the far side of the park
and turned toward Oro City, well before any more of
the gang came from the woods to look for their
partners.

———

Newt Morrison leaned on his pommel, forearms
crossed, as he watched their new recruit, a younger
man named Buck Smithers, and Bill Coogan free Jim
Flood from his bonds. He shook his head as he
watched, wondering about the collective intelligence of
this group. Their numbers had been whittled down
enough to put a crimp in their plans. What started as a
way to get rich in a hurry without having to work for it,
had become a deadly game with what was beginning to
appear as the work of one man. Flood sat up and
finished stripping off his bonds, sputtering and cussing
all the while. "I'm tellin' you that crazy galoot is huntin'
us down!"

"Whaddaya mean, huntin' us down?" questioned
Newt, sitting up straight and frowning at the wiggling
wort of a man.

"I'm tellin' you, he has all our names. He even read
off the names of those that started out with us from
Kansas an' have since been kilt or whatever!"

"Who'd he say was kilt?" asked Jerry Malcolm, who
sat his mount beside Newt Morrison.

"He said 'Doc' Jennison, Red Clark, ol' One-Eyed
Blunt, and uh, uh, Jim Lane. An' oh yeah, Dave Poole.
An'...he had Bill Tough an' Duncan Pitts on that list too!
I'm tellin' you, he's plum crazy an' he said to tell you

it'd be best to leave these mountains 'fore he comes lookin' fer the rest of us!"

"One man?!" growled Newt, "Are you sayin' yore willin' to tuck yore tail an' run from one man?"

Jerry Malcolm stood beside Flood, "Uh, that one man has killed eight of us, and as far as we know, he didn't have any help! An' if you think about it, Dave Poole had three or four that was ridin' with him back there in Kansas, so..." he shrugged.

"Near as I can figger, there was more. What about those two that rode with Blunt? What was their names, Judd Pollack an' the other'n. And it was the miner's court what done in Pollack. Don' know what happened to the other'n. An' like Jerry said, there were others that rode with Dave Poole." Newt shook his head, stepped down to look about the camp of Cord, mumbling as he kicked the pieces of the rocker box aside, and looked at the pick sticking out of the chest of Jack Hayes. He looked at the others, "But now, thanks to the miner's court, we have *his* name. Maybe we need to go on the hunt for him!"

16

STALK

After picketing his horse and pack mule in the trees near a likely looking clearing for a camp, Cord grabbed his rifle and with Blue at his heels, started back toward the bed of Tennessee Creek. When he left his diggings, he rode south along the creek, pushed through the willows into the creek, and rode back upstream on the gravelly bottom. He knew the outlaws would probably come looking for him, and he thought to completely cover his trail or at the least, confuse them a mite. He had purposely made it appear that he was headed back to Oro City, but when he came to a stretch of dry land thick with cacti and rocks, he cut through the willows to the creek. Now he was bound to do his best to wipe out any sign of his passing and especially any sign of his moving upstream and across the flats into the black timber on the east edge of the wide Tennessee Park.

He had intentionally kept himself busy, allowing little time to reflect and consider what was happening in his life. The last few weeks had been the most tumultuous of times, losing Bird - who he had begun to think

about as his possible lifetime mate, the run-ins with
several of the members of the Red Legs and the subse-
quent gunfights that resulted in his killing of several
men, and now? He shook his head as he crossed the
creek to the point in his trail where he turned into the
creek. With a quick look around, comfortable with the
thick willows and alders and berry bushes that stood at
least shoulder high and offered good cover, he went to
work to cover his tracks. He walked up the back trail
about twenty feet, and with a branch of a nearby sage,
began lightly dusting the tracks to have them appear to
fade from the wind, gradually making them disappear.
To give the appearance of time and wind, he walked
back along the tracks, using loose soil to drift from his
fingers and cover the tracks with dry soil as if the wind
had carried it. Carefully stepping from stone to stone or
behind cacti, he covered his trail satisfactorily, hoping
it would confuse or fool their tracker, but he was not
going to depend entirely on this ruse.

He moved back upstream, wading in the calf deep
water, and where he had ridden from the stream, he did
much the same to obscure those tracks, although he
had chosen to leave the stream where the terrain was
mostly flat moss-covered rock and left little or no sign
of his passage. He had kept to the willows and other
brush, but now he would have to leave the better cover
to make it across the flats to the trees and return to his
chosen camp. He turned back to look at the back trail
and his former encampment at his diggings and saw
dust rising. He doffed his hat, tiptoed to look over the
brush, and saw several riders coming from his former
camp. They were on his trail! He watched for a few
moments, saw they were riding at a good canter and

not paying close attention to the tracks before them. He grinned, hoping he had fooled them into believing he was headed back to town, and they were intent on catching him before he made it to town to report any of the happenings. When they rode past the point where he had turned into the creek, he slowly grinned, satisfied with his handiwork and turned back to his camp.

As he ducked and dodged through the brush and across the flats, his mind returned to his thoughts of reflection and the words of his father as he quoted the scripture continued to haunt him...avenge *not yourselves, but rather give place unto wrath: for it is written, Vengeance is mine; I will repay, saith the Lord...* "Yeah, Pa, but I also remember you preaching from Deuteronomy where it said somethin' like *I will render vengeance to mine enemies and will reward them that hate me. I will make mine arrows drunk with blood, and my sword shall devour flesh;* and I remember you sayin' somethin' about *If the foundations be destroyed, what can the righteous do?* And I remember you sayin' that meant the good people have to stand against the evil people and if we don't the *foundations* of our nation will be destroyed, then what? Remember that?" he shook his head as he realized he was talking out loud to a dead man, and looked around to see if there was anyone or anything that listened, but his only listener was a houn'dog named Blue who looked at him with his head cocked at an angle and a confused look on his face. Cord chuckled, stopped and went to one knee beside his very tolerant dog and rubbed him behind his ears and laughed.

He looked around, saw a rocky escarpment and quickly mounted it, looked through the black timber toward the trail that led back into Oro City, but the only sign was a bit of lingering dust in the air, and he was satisfied that the outlaws had ridden into town to look for him. He returned to his camp where the grulla and mule were picketed and began stripping off the gear and making a comfortable camp. He thought he would stay here, out of sight, and give some thought as to his plans and the coming days and what to do about the remaining outlaws.

His camp was in the bottom of a saddle that lay on the shoulder of a butte that held a talus slope facing south and speckled with aspen. Below him to the west, lay a thicket of aspen that rode the draw of a spring-fed creek. With his campfire circle beneath the broad branches of a big spruce to filter any rising smoke, rocks below and above him, and moss-rock formations on either side, Cord was pleased with his camp. It overlooked the East Fork of the Arkansas River, and beyond the river lay low-rising timber-covered buttes that sheltered the layout of Oro City, about two miles away, and the many diggings of California Gulch.

Cord built his hat-sized cookfire, hung the last of his venison steak strips on willow withes over the fire, pushed his coffee pot nearer the flames, pushed the Indian Potatoes into the coals, and sat back to await his feast. He dozed off with his fingers intertwined over his chest, his hat over his eyes, and leaning against the big trunk of the spruce. His legs were outstretched, his moccasined feet toward the fire. He considered himself a light sleeper and was confident in his selection of the campsite and felt secure, but no sooner had his eyelids dropped, than the snap of a dry stick brought him instantly awake.

He had long ago disciplined himself not to jerk

awake but just open his eyes slowly and look around
before moving, but the surprise made him jerk slightly,
and a gravelly voice said, "Easy now, nothin' to be
'feared of, I'm peaceful."

Cord slowly opened his eyes, pushed back his hat,
and stared at a sourdough that looked to be as old as
the mountains and about as dirty. But a grin split his
whiskers and mischief danced in his eyes as he began to
chuckle, "Seen ya crost the valley, watched you all the
way hyar, I did. You ain't bad fer a tenderfoot, but I seen
it right off, yup, din't know what'chu was doin' with
that thar rocker box, nor much else. Yup, you could use
some teachin' an' I'se just the man to do it."

"Who're you an' what're you doin' here?" growled
Cord, sitting up and glancing to the sizzling steaks.

The old-timer reached for the coffee pot, held it up
as if asking a question, and at Cord's nod, poured
himself and Cord full cups of steaming black brew. "I'm
called Cracker, Cracker Tibbs. Been in these hills
longer'n most ever'body, I'se one o' da' first, I was,
yessir."

"Did'ju get any gold?"

"Ummhmm, know's whar thar's more, too."

"Why aren't you out gettin' it, makin' your pile,
retirin' to the city?" asked Cord, sipping on the hot
coffee.

"Don' like the city, too many folks wit' thar' fingers
in yore pockets," drawled the grinning old man as he
reached into the pocket of his canvas trousers and
brought out a silver-inlaid briar pipe and began to
tamp some tobacco taken from a tin with the name J.R.
Green, into the bowl of the pipe.

"Ain't that what's happenin' hereabouts?" asked Cord.

"Ain't in my pockets. Ain't got none! Pockets that is, Hehehehe..." cackled the old rooster.

His holey canvas trousers were held up with a pair of worn galluses that stretched over his grey homespun shirt. A floppy felt hat, the brim at the front pinned back to the crown and giving a clear look at the whiskery face. Grey whiskers almost hid his ears for they too had long hair growing and moving in the breeze, the beard covered the neck of his shirt, but when he twisted around to reach for a stick to catch fire and light his pipe, faded longjohns showed. The sleeves were rolled up to expose most of his muscled forearms and it was easy to see, this man, although he looked as old as the hills, might not be so old and was definitely in good shape. Broad shoulders stretched the homespun, a narrow waist told of a trim physique, and the hobnail boots, although scuffed, were in good condition. This man was more than he pretended to be, and Cord glanced over his coffee cup at his visitor.

"So, what'chu up to, youngster? It's plain you ain't prospectin' and you handled them outlaws like you was a lawman or sumpin', so...what are you?"

17

MENTOR

CORD CHUCKLED, FINISHED HIS COFFEE AND REACHED FOR THE pot to pour another cup. He glanced at the steaks, sat the coffee pot and his cup down, grabbed one of the willow withes and extended it to Cracker. The old man grinned, licked his lips, and happily accepted the offering. Cord said, "There's a couple taters in the coals, go ahead an' drag one out for yourself."

Cord grabbed the second steak, used a stick to do as Cracker did, and dragged a potato from the coals. Cracker placed his potato on a rock beside him and carefully using his big Green River knife, he split it open and scooped out a dab and licked it off the blade, grinning and nodding. Cord did much the same and the two enjoyed the meal and the company.

As they were finishing eating, Cord asked, "Since you been around these parts a long time, has there been any recent robberies, you know, prospectors being robbed of their gold, maybe gettin' killed in the doin'?"

Cracker leaned back against a big boulder behind him and wiped his face, picked up his pipe and relit it, grinned at Cord, "Wal now, let me tell you a story 'bout this country." He began to relate the history of the nearby mountains and the many men that combed the countryside for gold or silver. He told of the settlers that sought to make money off the prospectors, like the merchants, barkeeps, and such like. "An' where ever you have gold, thar's them that digs it, an' them that wants it. Those that want it, are usually too lazy and think themselves too smart to dig it, instead they just wanna take it from those they see as weaker'n them."

He puffed thoughtfully on his pipe, letting the smoke curl past his hat brim, and leaned forward, "Now, there's allus a few o' them types, but mostly there's good folks in the gold huntin' bizness. There've been a few that tried, most were caught, tried in miner's court, like the one you was at, an' if found guilty, they hang 'em. That kinda discourages those that are not too prone to do their own diggin' and thinkin' 'bout stealin'. But..." he paused, frowned at Cord from under his bushy brows, and added, "That bunch you had a run-in with, I'm thinkin' they're up to no good. Why else would scamps like that be hangin' around hyar an' hidin' out in the hills?"

"Were there any others? Like them, I mean," asked Cord, leaning forward and squinting at the man through the smoke.

"Not that I know of, there ain't been. That's why it was so easy to get the miner's court together th' other day." He puffed on his pipe, sipped some coffee and looked up at Cord, "So, you're after 'em, are ya?" He paused, waiting for Cord to reply, but added, "You a lawman or sumpin'?"

"No, not a lawman, just a man huntin' justice for his family."

"Wal, I thot all that there stuff them Red Legs and such did was durin' the war?"

"This was after the war ended. They came down on our farm, killed everyone, stole livestock and everything they thought had value, burnt the place an' ran off," growled Cord, remembering every moment of the attack he had witnessed from the woods.

"You been after 'em that long?" asked the incredulous old-timer.

"That's why I asked if there was a sheriff or some other lawman around."

Cracker nodded his head slowly, looking at Cord with a slightly suspicious glint in his eye. "What'd yore pa do in the war?"

"That's just it. He wasn't in the war. My pa was a pastor of the local church, been there since 'fore the war started. Planned to spend the rest of his life there, but I'm sure he thought it'd be longer," grumbled Cord, shaking his head and reaching for the coffee pot.

Cracker chuckled as Cord frowned at him, "Oh, don't get all riled up, young'un. I'se laughin' cuz I tried that a spell, preachin' I mean. Did alright for a while, but that whole idee of livin' a life of poverty and humility, just din't fit the likes of me. Oh, I believe the Bible an' all that, an' I thought I was called to the ministry, studied up for it an' all, but...just din't fit, hehehehe."

Cord showed humor in his eyes as he responded, "Well, seems like you're doin' the poverty part pretty well, course I can't say 'bout the humility, but that seems to have been laid aside also."

"Hehehehe..." cackled the old sourdough, wiping

the coffee and leftovers from his whiskers. "But'cha know, just a short while back, there was a lawman through here, said he'd be comin' back ever' now'n then. He was one o' them new Colorado Rangers."

"Rangers? I heard of the Texas Rangers, but Colorado Rangers?"

"That's right, he seemed to be a right sort'a fella, showed me his badge an' ever'thin'. Said they was just like the Texas Rangers and were recruitin' and if'n I knowed anybody to send 'em his way. Cain't say as I know anybody that'd give up prospectin' to put on a tin badge," he mumbled, glancing up at Cord.

"Well Cracker," began Cord as he sat down his cup and stood to stretch, "if'n you're gonna be sharing this camp, you might wanna get your bedroll. It's gettin' late an' I'm for gettin' some rest."

Cracker stood, stretched, and walked bowlegged into the trees, over his shoulder he called, "Be right back, gotta get Mabel an' muh gear!"

When Cracker returned, he picketed Mabel, his mule, with Kwitcher and the pack mule, both of which eyed Mabel a bit suspiciously, but Cracker picketed the mule well away from the others. He dropped off his gear at the edge of the camp before tending to the animal. He hummed or whistled all the while he made his camp and Cord was surprised to see the old man stretch out a canvas cover and tie it taut to nearby trees, offering a dry camp for his bedroll. He sat a dutch oven near the cookfire, a pannier with other pans and such and a clay jar of sourdough. He looked up at Cord, "I'll be makin' us some fine biscuits fer breakfast. Got'ny thing to go with 'em?"

"Got a little pork belly left…" drawled Cord, looking at the doin's of the sourdough.

"Got'ny Indian 'tatoes left? We can cook them in the coals, fry up the bacon, and with the biscuits, we should do alright."

Cord nodded, grinning, and went to his bedroll, and with the humming and the whistling of Cracker, Cord was soon asleep, Blue at his side.

———

BEFORE FIRST LIGHT, Cord rolled from his blankets and with Blue at his heels, took a faint game trail to the top of the butte that overlooked the valley of the East Fork of the Arkansas. Below him rose the tops of a thick growth of aspen, making a faint green rolling carpet in the midst of the black timber. Off his left shoulder the slow-rising sun was separating the cotton-puff clouds from the mountaintops by painting the morning sky in pale shades of gold. Although he had not been very regular with his morning time of reading and prayer as he had done as a youth, he was determined to renew that practice. Cord sat on a flat rock that held him above the treetops on the south-facing slope, and cracked open his Bible. Most of the night, he tossed and turned with the enemy of sleep being the haunting strains of *Vengeance is mine, I will repay, saith the Lord.*

He thought of his father and the many times he spoke from the pulpit, but often explained his thoughts in more detail to his son. He frowned as he remembered something about a time when the Edomites exercised vengeance upon Judah, and God was not happy with them, although He said He also would bring vengeance.

But because they did it with a despiteful heart, seeking to destroy Judah for an old hatred, He promised to bring *great vengeance with furious rebukes on them so they would know He is the Lord.*

Cord flipped through the pages of his Bible until he came to the book of Ezekiel and chapter twenty-five and began to read the story of God's vengeance. He shook his head as he remembered his father saying, "So, son, when you harbor hatred in your heart, and think you have to bring vengeance because of that hatred, you're going against God's will and His way."

Cord let a heavy sigh lift his chest as he gritted his teeth and looked across the valley. Gold lances came from the rising sun and stretched across the sky above, coating everything below with a touch of gold. Cord chuckled to himself, thinking that's probably all the gold he would ever see or enjoy. He finished his time in prayer, asking God for his guidance and direction for his life and with a last glance to the Book, he chuckled as he rose, remembering the account from Luke how the enthusiastic disciples, James and John, saw others rejecting Christ and they asked, *Shall we command fire to come down from heaven, and consume them as Elijah did?* As he walked down the trail, he thought, *"Oh, if only..."*

"So, you think that bunch that hit your diggin's is a part o' them Red Legs?" asked Cracker, as he busied himself with the sourdough, rolling and punching it and stretching it out to cut the biscuits. He glanced to Cord when the younger man did not immediately respond. Cord had just returned from his solitary time with the Lord and His Word, trying to reconcile Justice and Vengeance.

Cord looked up at the old prospector, "I know they were." He slipped his paper of names from his pocket, "I've been keepin' score and I've got their names. Now, there are a couple new men in their ranks, but there's nothin' to say they're not just as bad as the rest."

Cracker mulled it over a little, glancing often to Cord who seemed to be deep in thought, then asked, "So, what makes what you're doin' any differ'nt than what they done? Seems to me you be huntin' men, without a license and on top o' that, I don't think there's an open season on men, even bad 'uns! Hehe-he," he cackled at his own joke but with a wary glance toward Cord. He looked at Cord, nodded toward his packs, "O'er there, in that first pack, there's a book, it's big and black and has the name on the cover of *Commentaries on the Laws of England; by Sir William Blackstone.* It's been used for years, both o'er there and here in America. The founders used it as a guide to write the laws of our land. Go get it and look it over, you might find it interestin'."

18

DIRECTION

They finished their breakfast and Cord kept glancing to the book and Cracker bided his time, letting the wonder stew in Cord's mind. When Cracker noisily sipped the last of his coffee, he grinned and said, "I'll save you some time. There's a page 'bout halfway through, that's dogeared. It starts with...that *the whole...* see it?"

Cord had snatched up the book and greedily flipped the pages to find what Cracker suggested. He looked up to the old codger, grinning, "Found it!"

"Read it, then."

"...*that the whole should protect all its parts, and that every part should pay obedience to the will of the whole; in other words, that the community should guard the rights of each individual member, and that (in return for this protection) each individual should submit to the laws of the community; without which submission of all it was impossible that protection could be extended to any.*"

Cord looked up, "Well the way that reads, we're supposed to protect each other, and that tells me that

I've got a responsibility to hunt 'em down, if not for me, for the rest of what he calls here the *community!*"

"Ummhmm, but if you read further, you'll see that the power of the community can be given to the individual and he lists the qualities needed for that individual."

Cord continued reading and when he came to what he thought Cracker meant, he began to read it out loud. *"...in whom those qualities are most likely to be found... attributes of Him who is emphatically styled the Supreme Being; the three grand requisites...of wisdom, of goodness, and of power; wisdom, to discern the real interest of the community; goodness, to endeavor always to pursue that real interest; and strength, or power, to carry this knowledge and intention into action."* Cord sat quiet, eyes going glazed as he considered what he had read. He looked at it again and again, re-reading and pondering. He looked up to Cracker with a question on his face and the old man responded with a chuckle.

"So ya' see young'un, it ain't all bad what'chu been doin', ya' just need to get it right an' do it for the right reasons and with the authority of the *community* behind you."

"Community? What would that be?" asked Cord.

"Wal, the way I see it, Lake County ain't got a sheriff, an' they don't rightly know what to do, ain't nobody in'trested in the job. And the county seat has moved from Oro City to Lourette, to Dayton, an' just this year to Granite. So by my thinkin', the onliest way to have any real authority is to be a Ranger or maybe a Federal Marshal or sumpin' like that."

"So, how does one become one of those?" asked Cord.

"I reckon the man you oughta be talkin' to is Dave Cook. He comes through here ever' now'n then. He's been all them things, even had his own detective agency, like the Pinkertons. He's been around to keep the miners in line, guard gold shipments, an' such. I reckon it's 'bout time fer him to show up again."

Cord stood, stretched, grinned at Cracker, "Well, until that time, I reckon we're gonna need some meat, so I'm goin' huntin'. I saw lotsa sign of elk back in the trees yonder, maybe they got a graze or bed o'er that saddle yonder."

"I'd eat some elk, yessir! An' while you're off gala-vantin' in the woods, I think I'll just meander down to town, see if'n I can find out anythin' 'bout Marshal Cook."

"Might listen for any doin's by the Red Legs too," grumbled Cord. He shook his head, went to his horse and mule and began saddling and rigging the two for his elk hunt.

———

THE EARLY MORNING sun stretched the shadows of the tall spruce across the trail followed by Cord. The game trail hugged the crest of a long ridge that pointed to the distant Buckeye Peak that stood as the leader of the cavalcade of mountain peaks that some were calling the Mosquito Range. With the lower flanks painted by patches of quakies with their fluttering pale green leaves, and several high country parks, this was ideal elk country. The trail dipped through a low saddle that was dimpled with scattered pines, but nothing moved. Cord pushed on and after about a mile of slow climbing, the trail broke into the open on a shoulder of the higher peak. Scattered bristlecone pines leaned as if pointing to the lower meadows, pink bark showing against the frigid winds, long-armed branches waving with the breeze. Cord guessed he was close to 12,000 feet, where the only trees were the bristlecone pine, and the only plants were the ground-hugging lupine and penstemon.

Cord stepped down, binoculars in hand, and sat on a cold rock to scan the lower parks and meadows. Blue came beside him, leaning against Cord for comfort, then sat down to wait. Cord grinned, lifted the binoculars and began to systematically search the many clearings and parks that lay below. He was at a point where a single ridge split two runoff draws that held several aspen covered slopes and parks. He slowly moved from one to the other, watching for movement or the telltale off-white rumps of the majestic elk. This was the time of year when the bulls would be sprouting their new velvet-covered antlers that would quickly grow to size, and most bulls would be separate from the cows that were probably calving or getting ready to drop their calves.

In the runoff to his left, he spotted movement and carefully searched the trees to find a good bunch of cows, some already with the orange-colored rambunctious calves at their side. He counted about a dozen cows, maybe half with calves, and all were lazily grazing on the tall grass in the meadow that straddled the little runoff creek. After a moment of watching the cows, Cord continued his search and scanning of all the parks. Across the ridge from the cows, and on the south-facing slope, he found what he wanted. A small herd of bulls, several showing their velvet-covered prongs that would soon branch and grow, some would grow as much as five or six feet from base to tip of the furthest prong, but now few had more than a spike or a single fork showing. He scanned the herd, saw several likely targets and then searched the hillsides for a possible trail that would get him closer and give him cover for shooting.

Satisfied, he mentally mapped out his trail, mounted up and slipped the Spencer from the scabbard, checked the loads, and satisfied, nudged Kwitcher to the trail, pulling taut the lead line of the mule and with Blue in the lead, they started into the black timber and his planned route to the lower park. It was an old game trail and in places, Kwitcher and the mule slid on their rumps as the loose soil did little to hold them back. Cord was laying back over the cantle of the saddle, the Spencer held at his chest, until the trail leveled a mite, and he regained his seat. He chuckled as he looked around, but knowing the clatter of hooves and the sliding rocks might give him away and spook the herd. He reined up, bending and twisting to see through the trees, but the herd still grazed.

Cord stepped down, rifle in hand and ground-tied Kwitcher and the mule, and with Blue at his side, he began his approach to the edge of the trees. The black timber-covered the north-facing slope and across the draw that held the little chuckling runoff creek, the rising sun bent its golden rays to paint the park on the south-facing slope and showcase the herd of bull elk. Some stood, heads up, looking about, perhaps having heard the rocks, but none were spooked. Cord stealthily moved beside a towering spruce with its grey smooth bark and went to one knee beside the trunk. The long branches stretched out, offering their shadow as cover and splitting just enough to provide Cord a view of the herd. He chose a young bull with smaller velvet-covered spikes that stood about a foot above the crown of his skull. His thick coat of dusty brown covered his sides and the dark mantle draped his neck and chest. He was grazing and Cord waited until he lifted his head, standing sideways to him, and with his sight on the lower chest behind his front legs, Cord squeezed off his shot.

The big Spencer bucked, roared, and spat lead and smoke. The blast reverberated across the draw, and as one, the herd jerked, and within moments the park was emptied of any living creature, but the single bull lay on its side, head downhill, unmoving.

Cord slowly stood, reached to his side to stroke Blue behind the ears, and said, "Well boy, now the work begins."

19

ORO CITY

The Eureka Tavern was the biggest and one of the last operating bars in Oro City, a town that at its peak numbered well over 10,000, now boasted only four hundred plus. The only other businesses that remained were the hotel, the livery, Best's eatery, and the mercantile, although there was an abandoned tavern that had been converted to a church that was only used when the circuit rider came into town. Several empty buildings stood as grave markers of the once boom town, some occupied by johnny-come-lately prospectors that were combining claims and working at sluicing, some resorting to ground sluicing. But the taverns were never at a loss for customers, both enthusiastic newcomer prospectors and the tired old sourdoughs, as well as the many followers. Several of such were gathered at the tables or standing at the bar, one foot hooked on the rail, a shot-glass in one hand keeping the other free for talking.

While in the corner, away from the windows, five men huddled at a table, talking in hushed tones, but watching everyone in the tavern, and listening to the many conversations. In the corner, a broad-faced, lantern-jawed man with dirty blonde hair sticking from under a tattered felt hat, rubbed his whiskery face and leaned on his elbows, looking around the table at the others, "Look, we know his name is Cordell Beckett, an' he's got whiskers, but we don' know much else. I think we oughta just watch for him, but go on with our bizness. I don't see no reason to curtail our bizness cuz o' one man." His raspy voice growled as he looked from one man to the other. To his left, the man known as Jerry Malcolm, who thought himself to be the number two man in the bunch, slowly shook his head with the mop of brown hair, ran his fingers through his hair and replaced his hat, looking around the table, "I dunno, boss, he done kilt a bunch of us, and not knowin' who he is, well..." he shrugged, glancing to the other three men and getting a couple nods in return.

James Flood had been leaning back in his chair, his knees on the edge of the table, dropped to all four legs of the chair and leaned forward, one arm on the table, the other at his side with his hand on the butt of his holstered pistol. "Wal, I'm thinkin' yore both right. We cain't be sittin' 'roun' doin' nuthin' and make money. We been listenin' to that bunch o'er at that table yonder 'bout their takin' twenty ounces this past week. That's what, three, four hunnert dollars? That's more'n we got all together! An' there ain't no bank hereabouts for 'em to put it in, so I'm thinkin' they need to put it in the bank of us'ns!" He grinned as he looked about the table, his comment eliciting several nods and grins, but they all looked warily at Newt Morrison, their self-appointed leader.

Newt leaned a little closer, lowered his voice and glared at James Flood, whose black hair and whiskers covered his face and more. Flood was a lean man, maybe six feet tall and all of a hundred fifty pounds, but his thin frame was misleading, for he was a strong man and quick with a gun, making him deadly as an enemy and a good man to have at your side as an ally.

Newt said, "Alright, Jim, then how's 'bout you follerin' that bunch, find out where their claim is, look it o'er and come back. Then we'll see about them makin' a deposit in the bank of us'ns!" he grinned a contagious grin as the others nodded and joined in the plan.

"By myself?" asked Flood.

Newt looked at the two newer men, Buck Smithers, a man that had tried prospecting and got nothing but blisters on his fat hands. His round featured face showed red cheeks, red bulbous nose, red ears, and sketchy whiskers everywhere else. His thinning brown hair did little to cover his dome that was crowned with a round top derby that matched his leather vest both in color and dirt. He sat beside Bill Coogan, the light-weight of the bunch that was maybe five foot six inches tall, and weighed in at less than a hundred fifty pounds. His oversized shirt did little to hide his slim features and his britches, hung loosely about his waist, held up by galluses that stretched over his linsey-Woolsey shirt. He was thin-faced, whiskers only on his chin, his nose had been broken in some long-ago bar brawl and pointed to his left, giving the impression he was looking that direction all the while.

"You two, Bill, Buck, you go with Jim, but don't go doin' nuthin' without him tellin' you, got it?"

Both men nodded, and with a glance at a rising Jim Flood, they scooted back their chairs and followed the man from the bar, leaving Newt and Jerry at the table. They had paid no attention to the old sourdough that leaned at the end of the bar, his whiskery face and tattered duds telling little of the man and definitely showing no prosperity. He had talked with another old-timer for a short while, but his attention had been focused on the conversation of the five men at the table in the corner, perfectly situated for their conversation, though muted and whispered, to be heard by the big ears of Cracker Tibbs. Cracker prided himself on his invisibility, that enabled him to move through town and taverns without notice, for he was no one important, never got in the way of others, and seldom talked, but was exceptionally good at listening. Only other old-timers knew him and all respected him.

Cracker placed a coin on the bar to pay for his drink and slowly shuffled out the door, glancing to the table of prospectors that had been talking about ground sluicing and the take in dust they had in the past week. These were the targets of the gang of former Red Legs and he thought to wait outside and give them a warning. Just outside the door, a long bench sat before the broad windows of the tavern and Cracker sat down, stretching his feet to the sunshine and with his hands clasped at his lap, he leaned back and closed his eyes just enough to appear to be napping, but slit enough to see what was necessary.

The three prospectors had risen from their table, started to the door and stepped out into the sunshine with only a glance to the man sitting on the bench. As they talked and decided to go to the eatery before returning to their claim, Cracker coughed and spoke just loud enough to get the nearest man's attention. The prospector turned, frowning, but Cracker motioned him to step closer and as the man started to sit down, Cracker spoke quietly, "No, just listen, but don't look this way. Those men in the corner were listening to you about your twenty ounces and they plan to hit your claim and take it. Three of 'em left 'fore you, and are waitin' to foller you. Just be warned, this bunch is dangerous."

The man slowly nodded, mumbled his thanks and quickly caught up with his two friends. As Cracker watched, he could tell the man was relating his warning as the other two looked back at the man on the bench. Cracker resumed his napping pose and with a heavy sigh, knew the men might heed his warning, but he doubted it. They were so confident in their luck at mining, they had begun to think themselves almost invincible and thought they could take care of themselves. But maybe not.

Cracker waited until the other two conspirators left the tavern, then rose and started to the mercantile. He planned on talking to Mike Densmore, the owner, and mine him for any news about Dave Cook or someone else of authority, thinking about the Rangers and others, someone that might be interested in recruiting Cord as a deputy. He was not too anxious to report to Cord about the plans of the gang, at least not until he found out about the possibility of gaining some authority for the man. Cracker laughed to himself, knowing he got more fun out of interfering in other's lives, helping to change their course, hopefully in a good way, and improving their lot. Gold was alright, but mighty cold and unsatisfying, but seeing people learn and grow and become a part of the community in a good way, that was something that lasted and was quite satisfying. He may not be a preacher anymore, but he could be a positive influence and he preferred doing it in an anonymous manner. He shuffled toward the mercantile, grinning to himself, thinking about his new friend Cord, and hoping good things would come of his friendship.

Cracker's good friend, Mike Densmore, often joined him in his conspiratorial ways of interfering in other's lives, both enjoying their antics and taking great satisfaction in what they did, even though it often went unacknowledged or recorded. When Cracker pushed into the darkened interior of the Oro City Mercantile, he stopped just inside the door, letting his eyes become accustomed to the lesser light, and spotting Mike behind the counter, pushed his way past the tables and more that held the displays of wares. Cracker waited to the side, appearing to examine the material of some canvas trousers, until Mike finished with his customer. As the man turned to leave, Mike glanced Cracker's way, smiled and motioned his friend near. Since the closing of the only bank, the mercantile had become both the post office and the bank for the remaining business in the town, and Mike served as both banker and postmaster. The two friends were soon leaning close, speaking in conspiratorial tones, chuckling and laughing, and making their plans for their manipulations.

20

CONSIDERATIONS

HE STOOD AT THE END OF THE BAR, HIS HAT BENT LOW, THE collar of his duster turned up, shadows covering his face. Cord leaned on his elbows, looking over the soiled copy of the Rocky Mountain News newspaper dated March something, 1868. The date had been smudged, but Cord knew it to now be sometime in mid-May, 1868. He frowned as he read the lead article, *Governor Hunt makes treaty with Utes*, it told about a new treaty negotiated with Kit Carson, Colorado Territorial Governor Alexander Hunt and several listed leaders of the Utes, with Ouray being the primary leader, but Cord recognized the name of Kaniache of the Capute Ute, the tribe that had been the home of his friend Yellow Singing Bird, the woman he had considered marrying, but was killed by the three men of the Red Legs down by Tincup.

He read further and saw the condition of the treaty required the Ute people to surrender all claim to the land east of the 107th west meridian, which basically meant surrendering most of the Rocky Mountains through central Colorado Territory. Cord shook his head and sighed heavily, remembering his time with the Capute Ute people, feeling bad for them. He continued to read with an occasional glance around the interior of the Eureka Tavern, but there were few others around. Two men nursed their drinks down the bar, three others were arguing over some worn-out playing cards, and two more sat silent at a corner table, staring into their empty glasses.

When Cord finished his hunt and had the elk hanging high in the trees at his camp, he picketed the mule, and went to town, hoping to find Cracker or at least learn something about the band of outlaws. Now he stood lonesome, reading, and reminiscing. As he read about how Central City had placed a bounty on Indian scalps, his attention was captured by an article headed, Colorado Rangers Make Arrests. He frowned as he read a lengthy article about the founding of the Rangers and the way they have been used. It spoke of a Schuyer Colfax and Samuel Bowles who had worked with other leaders, Thomas Gibson, George Monell, John Dailey and William Byers, to form a statewide law enforcement organization patterned after the Texas Rangers. They had asked Dave Cook to lead it, but he declined and the men leaned on Governor Hunt and his experience as a Federal Marshall to set up the group. They had already been successful in guarding many gold shipments from the mines, arrested some outlaws that conspired to steal the gold, and had assisted in the Battle of Glorieta Pass in the Civil War. Now they were active in Central City, Golden and other communities to the north. Cord turned the page just as a familiar voice spoke from the corner of the bar.

"Thought that was yore horse at the rail. You have any luck huntin'?" asked Cracker, motioning to the bartender to bring him a drink.

"Ummhmm, got an elk hangin'," answered Cord. "You learn anythin'?"

"Ummhmm, saw yore boys, they was goin' after some diggin's south o' town, but that was this mornin'. I warned the claim holders 'bout 'em, so…" he shrugged.

"Anythin' else?" asked Cord, pushing the paper aside and reaching for his mug of beer.

"Muh friend o'er to the Mercantile said one o' them rangers was due to come into town any day now, an' also he heard 'bout a federal marshal that's been makin' the rounds o' the minin' camps. But he don' know his name or when he'll show his face." Cracker drained the glass of the whiskey, wiped his face and motioned for the bartender to refill. He looked at Cord, spoke low, "He also said some o' the business people an' others been talkin' 'bout gettin' themselves a sheriff."

"Wal, I dunno much 'bout bein' a lawman, don't rightly know what I'd do. 'Sides, if'n I was to be a sheriff hereabouts, wouldn't that kinda require me to stick 'round here? Couldn't just up an' leave whenever I needed, now could I?"

"Prob'ly not. Mebbe we need to go back to camp. I allus thinks better on a full stomach, don'tchu?"

Cord chuckled, "Yeah, I reckon." He finished his beer, left a coin to pay, and looked at Cracker, "How 'bout we just meet up at camp? That way won't nobody know we're together."

Cracker nodded, pushed his glass around and leaned on the bar as Cord stood tall and walked from the room. He stepped onto the boardwalk, looked up and down the street, and went to the hitchrail to loose his grulla. As he swung aboard, he caught a glimpse of two men that sat in the shade of the overhang of the mercantile, they were watching him and they looked familiar. Cord nudged Kwitcher away from the Eureka, and started down the dusty street, his back to the two men as the big stallion stretched out and kept pace with Blue.

At the end of the street as it turned north, Cord glanced back up the street and saw the two men had left their perch and disappeared toward the livery. The main road from Oro City led west and followed the California Gulch, winding through the many structures of the claims and diggings of the miners. A lesser road bent to the north to cut through the timber and meet the Arkansas River. It was the lesser road chosen by Cord that would eventually join the trail on the north bank of the East Fork and eventually to the game trail that would take him to his camp. But Cord was not inclined to lead anyone to his camp and reined up behind the livery to await anyone that might be following. He was not disappointed when the two riders proved to be the same men that had watched him mount up and leave the Eureka. As they came around the corner of the livery, Cord spoke out, "Lookin' for somethin'?"

The two surprised riders quickly reined up and

faced Cord who sat with his rifle across the pommel, his hand on the grip and finger on the trigger. It was quickly noticed by the two who had reached for their pistols but stopped and slowly lifted empty hands to place them on their pommels, a weak grin splitting each face. The nearest man spoke.

"Uh, no, we was just leavin' town, need to get back to our camp 'fore dark," he explained.

"And where might that be?" asked Cord.

"Uh, the other side o' the river, north," he nodded with his head.

"Don'tchu fellas know it ain't polite to follow folks? Especially here in gold country. Fella can't help but be suspicious, you know, and when a fella like me gets suspicious, I just naturally grab a gun and start shootin'. But since you fellas are so polite an' all, I'll let it go, *this* time." He lifted the muzzle of the rifle, motioning the men to get moving and they quickly obliged. Cord sat watching as they took the trail into the trees and disappeared. He waited until he no longer heard the sound of hoofbeats, then nudged Kwitcher into the trees, away from the trail. He would make his own route back to camp, weaving through the timber and pine needle-covered ground that would obscure his passing. He knew the lay of the land and could easily cross the East Fork, take to the trees and work his way up the bluff and through the aspen to his camp. It gave him time to reflect on what he had read and what Cracker had said, but he still was a bit undecided about what he should do regarding his hunt for the outlaws. He was not about to give up on the idea of bringing justice down upon them, but he was a little tired of killing and hiding and had given thought about finding a better way to accomplish the same task.

When he came to the East Fork, he reined up on the south bank, leaned forward on the pommel and looked at the fast-flowing clear cold mountain water. Although mostly shallow, there were several undercut banks and deep pools behind the ripples around rocks, and he began considering something he hadn't done in a long time. He stepped down, ground-tied Kwitcher in the shade with some deep grass, reached into his saddlebags and brought out the fishing string, hooks, and his small spade. He went to the riverbank, found a likely spot and began digging for worms. Within moments he had several fat squirming worms and he put one on the hook, the line tied to a strong willow, and happily sat down on the bank, remembering the times he did much the same as a boy.

Within less than half an hour, he had a stringer of rainbow trout, and after cleaning them, he hung the stringer on his saddle horn and mounted up, crossed the shallows and took to the trees to return to camp. He was greeted by a surprised Cracker, "Wal, there you be. I was wonderin' what happened since you left 'fore I did."

Cord chuckled, lifted the stringer of fish, and stepped down, handed them to Cracker, and grinning, answered, "Had to relive some o' my youth!"

Cracker grinned, accepted the stringer and went to the fire ring, laid them on a flat rock and dug out his frying pan and a bag of cornmeal. He looked up at Cord, "We'll be eatin' fine this night! I got us some sweet taters at the mercantile, and already whipped up some biscuits," he nodded to the dutch oven sitting on some coals and with more coals on the lid.

Cord grinned, "Suits me! You make a man a mighty fine wife, Cracker!" he laughed.

Cracker grinned, "Aww shucks, don't go spoilin' me now!" as he rolled the fish in the cornmeal and lay them in the skillet.

21

CHANGE

CRACKER WAS PUTTERING AROUND THE FIRE WHEN CORD rolled from his blankets. Cord sat up, ran his fingers through his hair and squinted at Cracker who was whistling while he prepared the breakfast of pork belly, biscuits, and fried potatoes. Cord shook his head as he grinned, stood, and went to the creek to wash his face and freshen up a mite. When he returned to the fire, Cracker handed him a steaming cup of coffee and Cord grinned, "You're gonna spoil me, I'm tellin' you," and chuckled as he accepted the cup.

"Got som'pin' I wanna talk to you 'bout. Have a seat, an' I'll talk while I work."

Cord frowned, recognizing Cracker was a bit more serious than usual. But as Cord seated himself and lifted the cup, Cracker began to explain, "Since the slide of Oro City an' so many businesses closin' up and miners leavin', things have changed a bit. One o' those businesses that closed was the only bank we had, and the post office had to move to the mercantile. So did the bank. Now, Mike, he's the man at the mercantile, has been doin' the bankin' and such. The preacher, Reverend Dyer, John, he 'expresses' some o' the miner's gold to Denver City, when he carries the mail o'er to Fairplay an' Buckskin. But he don't like to carry much. So, Mike's been puttin' it in his safe an' tryin' to figger out what to do. I thought maybe we could get you to take it to Denver City and put it in the bank, exchange some for cash money, you know. Now, since you're new, and ain't been 'round much, there's no reason anyone'd think you'd be carryin' any gold, so..." he shrugged, looking to Cord with an expectant expression, hoping for an answer.

Cracker looked back to his frying pan, and continued, "But there's a couple other things you might wanna know. Some o' them fellers you been after, well they was seen headin' toward Mosquito Pass yesterday, and that's the way you'd be goin'. Also, the preacher, Reverend Dyer, he'd go with you as far as Buckskin, maybe even Fairplay or so, so you'd have comp'ny."

"You said a couple things?" asked Cord.

"Yeah, we was talkin' 'bout the law, you know, the Rangers, Marshal, an' such. Mike kinda likes the idea of you becomin' the sheriff, but if'n you go to Denver, you could stop in an' talk to the Rangers an' maybe even find out 'bout Marshal'n."

Cord sat back and sipped his coffee, looking through the rising steam at Cracker as he considered the proposition. As he sat still, mulling things over, Cracker added, "We'd pay you for the trip. It'd be worth, oh, maybe fifty dollars!" he grinned.

Cord frowned, "Fifty dollars? Why so much?"

"Wal, you'd be carryin' 'bout a hunnert, hunnert an'

fifty pounds o' gold dust," he muttered, looking at his cooking and avoiding the gaze of Cord.

"That's a lotta gold dust!" declared Cord, thinking about the amount, calculating about what it'd be worth, "That's over $65,000.00!" declared Cord, spilling his coffee and bringing him upright to glare at Cracker.

"Wal, I ain't sure he'd be sendin' the whole hunnert an' fifty pounds," shrugged Cracker, "It's just that it's been accumulating and he's gettin' short on currency," added Cracker, scraping some bacon and potatoes into a tin plate for Cord, and extended the offering to him.

"Well, even the hundred pounds would be close to $45,000!"

Cracker just nodded and filled his own plate. "That's why we'd just want you to do it, you know, a lone man, pack mule, lookin' like you ain't got more'n a couple dollars," he shrugged.

"I'll need to give it some thought," responded Cord, shaking his head that he would even consider such an endeavor, especially alone and with so many outlaws on the loose.

———

CORD HAD SPENT most of the day around camp, skinning out the elk, making some specialty cuts on the carcass to preserve the best cuts, making a smoke rack for smoking some of the meat, basically taking the time to give thought about the proposal from Cracker and his friend, the banker.

Cracker was reading one of the several books he packed with him, classics and more, and was stretched out, leaning on a log with one hand holding the book, the other behind his head. Cord saw the title of the book, *Gulliver's Travels*, by Jonathan Swift. He often chuckled as he read it, enjoying the momentary escape from his time.

Cord stepped close and said, "I'll take that journey for you and the banker, but there's two things necessary."

Cracker sat up, placed his book aside and looked at Cord, "Name 'em!"

"One, travelin' with the preacher is alright, but we leave tonight, after dark. And it'll be a hundred dollars instead of fifty."

"Fifty when you leave, fifty when you get back," replied Cracker, extending his hand to shake with Cord to seal the deal.

Cord nodded, shook hands and returned to his animals, set to prepare for the journey. He called back over his shoulder, "And any extra supplies I might need."

"Done!" replied Cracker.

Cord glanced to his smoke rack, noted the slow smoke was shrouding the strips of meat and he hoped they would be ready for his journey. He set about brushing Kwitcher and checking his gear. He would clean all his weapons, check his gear, brush the mule, and check the hooves of both the horse and mule, check the packs and anything else that came to mind. As he checked Kwitcher's shoes, he thought the rear shoes were a little too worn and it would be best to have new shoes all the way around. He told Cracker of the need and with a glance to the sun for the time, he nodded, saddled up and with Blue at his side and the pack mule on a taut line behind, he started on the shorter trail down to town and the livery.

Cracker took the longer way around, not wanting anyone to see that he and Cord were together, and went directly to the mercantile to meet with Densmore. He tethered his mule at the hitchrail in front, stepped into the darker interior and with a nod to his friend, he went to the displays and looked over the merchandise until Mike was alone. With a broad grin to his friend, he stepped closer, shook his hand and said, "He'll do it an' he wants to leave tonight. Figgers to put some miles behin' him after dark, an' he's fine with the preacher bein' with him."

"Good, good," declared Densmore. "Now we gotta get things packed." He looked around the store, thinking, and looked back to Cracker, "He takin' a pack mule?"

"Ummhmm, an' he's gonna need some prospectin' tools, he's got some, but I reckon he needs a shovel, a pick, mebbe another pan. Used ones if'n you got 'em."

Densmore nodded and began gathering the items, looked back at Cracker, "What kinda weapons he carry?"

"Hmmm, a Spencer, a Winchester, a coach gun, an' I think he packs a Colt Army pistol, converted to use those metal ca'tridges."

Densmore frowned, went behind his counter and started stacking some cartridge boxes of the .44 caliber on the counter, and with a glance to Cracker, "Both that rifle an' the pistol use these same cartridges." He picked a couple other boxes and placed them on the counter, "Those are for the Spencer and Coach gun." He pushed them to the side, looked up to see the preacher come into the store. "Howdy there parson, how you doin' this fine day?"

Reverend John Dyer grinned, nodded, "Fine Mike, fine, and you?" he glanced to Cracker, nodded, and back to Mike, "Got'ny mail to go o'er the hill?"

"I do, I do, an' there's more. Pull up a chair there by the stove an' we'll join you. Got somethin' you might be interested in, make you a little extra money."

"It's been so long since I had *extra* money, I wouldn't know what to do with it," answered the preacher, stepping closer to the stove and sliding a chair close.

After Mike and Cracker explained about Cord and his venture to take some gold to Denver, they added, "Now Cord's a good man, he just ain't never been o'er the route you know. He's kinda new to this country, an'...you might oughta know, he's kinda been on a vengeance trek, chasin' after some Red Legs that kilt his family and burnt their farm. Some of 'ems been sighted hereabouts, but...don't rightly know where they are now. You don' hafta go all the way to Denver City if you druther not, but get him o'er Mosquito Pass an' into the park, then he can find his way on," explained Cracker.

Mike added, "And like we said, we'll pay you some extra for doin' that, you know, more'n what you'd get for carryin' the mail."

"Extra?" asked the preacher, with a slight grin.

"Oh, another ten dollars, how's that sound?" asked Mike.

"Fine, gentlemen, fine," answered the preacher with a broad smile.

22

TRAVELING

THE MOON WAS WAXING FULL WHEN THE TWO MEN RODE away from the back door of the mercantile. It was a couple hours after sundown and the town had settled in for the night. The town was dark and the animals shuffled easily along, making little noise as they moved. The trail was a rough wagon road, occasionally used to transport goods over Mosquito Pass to the settlements in South Park, although shorter than the conventional route that would take them south and over Trout Creek Pass to Hartsel and was a good fifty to sixty miles further, it was a rough road that was more of a trail than a road.

As they left Oro City behind, the trail took them through a cut that followed Little Stray Horse Gulch between two timbered buttes and around a point, bent to the north and back to the east before dropping into Evans Gulch. The trail climbed the lower flank of Prospect Mountain, kept to the timber until bending around the shoulder of the foothill and climbed the east flank of the bald slopes of the mountain before turning back to the east.

They were only about five miles out of Oro City, but the wind from the north rolled over the ridge of Prospect Mountain and the preacher motioned Cord to the trees beside the trail. Once under cover, the preacher stepped down, motioned Cord to do the same and both men sat on a big rock with grass all around, allowing the animals a bit of a blow and some graze.

Preacher Dyer looked at Cord, "We're about to start a pretty good climb, thought the horses could use a breather 'fore we start."

Cord nodded, leaned back on his elbows and looked at the stars. It was a clear night and the many constellations strutted their stuff overhead. Cord pointed, "Isn't that Orion, the great hunter?" he asked as he looked heavenward.

The preacher looked where Cord pointed, nodded, "Yes, I believe it is. *There is one glory of the sun, and another glory of the moon, and another glory of the stars: for one star differeth from another star in glory.* I Corinthians 15:41." He chuckled as he looked back at Cord who was staring at him.

"You remind me of my father. He was good at that, coming up with a scripture to fit whatever we were talking about."

"Your father was a man of the cloth?" asked the preacher.

"He was a pastor for all the years I knew him, but before that he was a soldier," answered Cord, "So his advice was usually pretty sound as he drew from both parts of his life."

"Sounds like you had a good childhood. Were you often in church?"

"It was, my childhood, that is, it was good. And yes, we were in church every time there was anything goin' on, until..."

"Until?" asked the preacher, frowning as he looked at Cord.

"It's a little longer story. Maybe we better get back on the trail and make some time while we can."

The preacher nodded, and both men stepped back aboard to resume their journey. Within moments they were clear of the trees as the trail cut across the bald face and a talus slope of the long shoulder ridge that fell from the higher Mount Prospect. It was a bald saddle crossing that pointed the way to the long razor-back ridge that marked the trail that would climb to the crest. When they hit the saddle crossing, merciless winds came from the north, whipping over the saddle, carrying the needles of ice and snow that drove into the exposed skin of their faces and necks. Both men hunkered into their coats, lifting collars and jamming hats down tight on their head. They lifted neckerchiefs to cover their faces and pulled hands back into their sleeves as they bent over their pommels and leaned into the wind. The horses lowered their heads, turning their faces away from the wind, and plodded onward to the rugged climb that lay before them. The moon was bright and muted shades of gold reflected off the snow-drifts that clung to every cut, every dip, every crevice. The trail was marked by the lines of white where even the tracks on the trail caught the drifting snow and ice.

From the beginning of the saddle crossing to the base of the climb was less than half a mile, but it was most of an hour in the crossing. When they hit the trail that marked the beginning of Mosquito Pass, the track bent to the south and put their backs to the wind and the horses picked up the step with the wind whipping their tails around them and for about two hundred fifty yards, they had a slight relief, but at the crest of a sharp drop off the trail bent back to the north and they once again faced into the wind as the trail slowly bent to the east as it climbed the steep slope. Another switchback and their backs were to the wind, but only until the trail made another switchback and so it went as they slowly climbed higher. The wind howled and moaned as it rose from the long valley below and whipped its way to the crest of the long ridge that held the pass. From the last switchback that put them facing the wind, the trail continued just below the crest of the ridge for most of a mile before making another steep climb and reaching the crest. Once over the lip of the crest, the wind abated and the men sat up, dusted the clinging snow and ice off their coats and stopped to let the horses have a short breather.

When they pushed on the trail held to the east face of the long bald talus slope that fell from the long ridge before breaking over another narrow saddle to cross a razorback ridge that marked what the preacher called London Mountain. From that ridge down to the Mosquito Draw was about two miles, but the shelter of the draw and the heavy timber was a welcome sight. The preacher pushed into the trees to a familiar camp-site and stepped down. He looked at Cord, "Sun'll be comin' up soon, thought we could get some rest, let the animals have some graze," he motioned to the deep grass around, "and the deep pine needles make for a good sleepin' mat."

"Sounds good to me, and I'm all for some hot coffee. It'll probably be a week 'fore I get warm after all that!" declared Cord. "But first, the horses..." he ducked under the low branches and went to the animals to begin stripping the gear. He started brushing the stallion, talking all the while to the animals. "There now, boy. I'll get this ice and snow from your coat, an' then you can roll in the dirt an' I'll brush you again!" He chuckled as he worked, looking from the stallion to the mule and down to Blue who stood beside him, his coat heavy with ice and snow as he shivered, waiting his turn for attention.

"Ah, but this is fine weather," declared the preacher as he brushed the thick coat of his bay gelding. "You should cross this pass in the winter!"

"In the winter? You cross this pass in the winter?" asked an incredulous Cord, frowning at the preacher, "Why?"

The preacher chuckled, "To carry the mail and to preach to the people. They need the warmth of the gospel in the midst of the cold of winter. That's when I can preach about the fires of hell and they both get warm and convicted!" he laughed as he stepped back from the bay and let the big animals roll in the dirt and grass. He watched as the horse twisted and rolled as if scratching his back, then stood and shook, looked to the preacher for more attention.

When they finished with the animals, both men walked into the clearing, carrying branches and other firewood. Cord dropped his armload, watched as the preacher laid the fire and asked again, "So, in the winter?"

The preacher chuckled, "Ummhumm," he sat back, pointed to the tall spruce and said, "Look there," and pointed to a break in the branches high overhead.

Cord frowned, leaned back to look where the preacher pointed and saw high up, where some branches had been broken off and a stretch of the grey trunk stood bare. He shaded his eyes as he looked with the faint light of early dawn showing the image, and he spotted what appeared to be a carved cross, cut into the bark, leaving a dark scar on the trunk. On one side of the cross was the letter J and on the other a D. He looked down at the preacher who was grinning as he watched Cord's reaction.

"You carved that?" asked Cord.

The preacher nodded, returned to his laying in of the fire, "That was three winters ago."

"But that's, that's three times my height!"

"More like four," answered the preacher, then continued, "That winter the snow, down in the draw there, was more'n twenty feet deep. Here in the trees, well, I was sitting down on my snowshoes when I carved that. I did that so folks'd know I had been here, just in case I didn't make it out."

Cord shook his head, looking from the preacher and back to the carving. He looked about the camp and the area where they were, wondering if they were as alone as he felt. The preacher said, "We'll have our meal and coffee, and by then it'll be light. But the horses are tired as are we, so we'll move further down, deeper into the trees, before we sleep."

23

ALMA

The soul-piercing scream drove through the trees and across the draw. The horses sidestepped nervously, heads high, ears pricked, and nostril flaring. The mule lifted his head, snorted, facing the direction of the scream as Cord came from his blankets as if launched on a spring. He stood, feet apart, rifle in hand, searching the trees, as the scream diminished into several snorts and coughs. He looked at the preacher who was sitting up, still in his blankets, and grinning at Cord.

Cord shook his head and asked, "What was that!?"

The preacher chuckled, tossed aside his blankets, and stood, "That, my friend, was what old-timers call a catamount, but most folks call a mountain lion or panther. When you can hear 'em, they're just sounding a warning. It's when you know they are there, but can't hear 'em that you need to be concerned. That one sounded like he came from higher up in the rocks, maybe atop this ridge, too far to worry about. But watch your mule, they know more'n most and mules are great killers of mountain lions."

Cord relaxed, walked around the camp and picked up some branches and twigs to make a fire for some coffee. With a glance at the sun, he guessed it to be just shy of noon. "Reckon we better get on the move, got a long way to go today."

"Well, you maybe, but not me. I'm just goin' in to Alma, get some folks together, hold services. Then maybe on to Fairplay and do it again."

As Cord poured the coffee, the preacher looked at him and asked, "So, Cord, how's things with you and the Lord?"

Cord frowned, poured his own coffee and sat back on the big rock and looked over the cup at the preacher, "Whadaya mean preacher?"

"Oh, I think you know, seein' as how you were raised in a home where your daddy was a preacher. What I mean is, have you ever made that important decision and asked Jesus Christ to be your Saviour, you know, have you received that free gift of eternal life like it says in Romans 6:23?"

Cord dropped his eyes, took a sip of the hot brew and looked at the preacher, "Yeah, I did that, but that was before."

"Before?"

"Ummhmm, before those Red Legs came through and killed my family and burnt the farm, and before I took to their trail and caught some, killed some. Yeah, before all that," he shook his head, staring into his cup and remembering.

"So, are you thinking all that made a difference? Changed things somehow?"

"Well doesn't it? Ain't it wrong to hate, and kill?"

"Well, it does say *Thou shalt not kill,* but that doesn't have anything to do with your salvation."

Cord frowned, thought about it a little, then asked, "Could you explain that for me?"

"Certainly. You see, salvation is a gift, no strings attached, no conditions, you don't have to earn it, pay for it, or anything like that. It's not based on what *you* do, it's all in *His* Word. Like in Romans 8:35-39 where he tells us that *nothing* can separate us from the love of God which is in Christ Jesus our Lord. It's like this, you see in John 10:27-29 He says we are in Christ's hand," the preacher held out his hand and pointed to his palm, then closed that hand like he held something in it and put it in his other hand, "then He says we are in the Father's hand, and in Ephesians 4:30 He adds that we are sealed by the Holy Spirit!" He brushed his free hand over the closed fist like a seal. "So, for anything to get to us, down deep inside there, first he has to break the seal of the Spirit, then pry off the Father's hand, and then pry open Christ's hand." He chuckled, "Ain't nuthin' gonna get to us there." He sipped his coffee, saw a look of confusion on Cord's face and added, "It also says in I Peter 1:2-5 and in II Timothy 1:12 that we are *kept* by the power of God.

"Now, don't get me wrong, Cord. God doesn't want us goin' about doing wicked things, but he does say if we make a mistake, do something wrong, stub our toe, that He stands ready to accept our plea and our asking for forgiveness and is eager to help get us back on the right track. None of us are perfect, we all make mistakes, but when we do, all we need to do is go back to Him and ask for forgiveness, and it is ours."

"So, what should I be doing?"

The preacher chuckled, "That's between you and God. But I recommend you go to the book of Ephesians chapter four and start practicing a few of those things that are listed there and in the next chapter, it's all about how we should be living. But...remember, you're not perfect, you're still going to make some mistakes, but like your friend said, one of the first things you need to get settled is your current battle with vengeance and justice, and that'll start if you get on the right side of the law."

———

THEIR CAMP LAY in the thick timber that shrouded the flank of a steep talus slope that fell from the ridge high above them. The ridge, the shoulder from Loveland Mountain, pointed to the east and tapered off into the trees. Cord and the preacher followed the game trail that meandered through the timber but kept the little stream known as Mosquito Creek always in sight below them. The ridge tapered off after a couple miles and Mosquito Gulch widened into a valley about a mile across. The timber was sparse, most having been cut for cabins and sluices by the many prospectors. With the low ridge to their left and a higher finger butte on their right, the preacher pointed to the remains of several cabins, "That's what was called Sterling although some just called it Mosquito, and across the valley was Park City, those two, three cabins are all that's left. When the gold played out, most scattered, some o'er the hill yonder," pointing to the ridge on their left, "to Buckskin, originally called Buckskin Joe after a big black man that always wore buckskins. Now Buckskin was purty big in its day, some said it had 'bout five thousand people, several businesses, couple hotels, eight or ten taverns, and more. Now it's just empty buildings, a few thick-headed prospectors, but most folks consider it to be another ghost town. And down the draw from there was Dudley and Alma. Dudley's empty, but Alma's still goin'. I'll be stoppin' there to have services for the folks."

They rode a little further, having covered a little more than three miles since they left camp, and the preacher pointed to their left, "I'll be takin' that trail o'er to Alma. Yer best route would be to follow this'n," pointing to the wagon road they now followed, "down to the mouth of Mosquito Creek. There's another ghost town called London Junction there. Go south about four, five miles and you'll come to Fairplay. There's a hotel there and such, if you're of a mind to stay in one, or you can turn back to the north and follow the stage road all the way to Denver City. It's about four, maybe five days on to Denver City."

"And if I don't stay in Fairplay?"

The preacher grinned, leaned on his pommel, "Well, if you head north out of Fairplay, after 'bout four miles you'll cross over Red Hill and on the north face, there's thick timber and good places to camp. Plenty of graze for your animals and a good creek, Trout Creek, down in the bottom. So, you could stay on the hill or keep goin' 'bout a mile to the creek and there's places thereabouts."

Cord turned to face the preacher, extended his hand, "Well, preacher, I reckon this is goodbye, and I thank you for the company and the counsel."

The preacher grinned, accepted Cord's hand and said, "Let's have a word of prayer if we may?"

He held Cord's hand and began to pray, thanking God for the time together and asking for His guidance and protection for Cord as he traveled. After the "Amen" the men nodded and parted ways. Cord remained on the trail, watching the preacher take to the lesser road and start over the ridge. When he passed from sight, Cord nudged Kwitcher and they started east on the trail following Mosquito Creek. When he came to the ghost town that had been known as London Junction, a sign pointed to the south that said "Fairplay four miles."

Fairplay lay above the confluence of Beaver Creek and the Middle Fork of the South Platte River. The flats were an ancient alluvial plain that lay between the waterways at the point of the long ridge that pointed back to the high mountains. Fairplay had been founded by some late comers to the area that missed out on some of the larger and more productive claims in the area and as they gathered together, they wanted a fair way that all could get reasonable claims. They wanted fair play, thus the name of the town. While so many others had become empty ghost towns and had been robbed even of many buildings, some of those same structures found a home in Fairplay and the town was growing as the nearby claims were profitable and oper-ating. Cord rode slowly through the town, thought there were too many people and chose to keep moving.

24

<hr style="width:15%">

RED HILL

BECAUSE OF THE TIMES AND THE PLACE, EVERYONE THAT WAS not known was looked upon with suspicion and what Cord did not know was that the distrust of strangers was well warranted. There had been several claims robbed, prospectors killed, and pokes stolen. It was recent happenings and any new face fell under suspicion, but Cord kept moving and put Fairplay and the gold fields behind him, yet often checked his back trail due to his own concerns and suspicions. It was late afternoon when he turned north on the stage road that would take him to Denver City and he saw no other travelers.

The road twisted around and between two low-rising buttes, dipped through a no-name feeder creek that fed Crooked Creek, and at the crest of the second rise, Cord stopped, twisted around in his saddle to check his back trail and thought he saw a pair of riders, but they dropped from sight behind a low knoll. He nudged Kwitcher to cross Crook Creek and with heavy patches of pale green leafed aspen on the lower flanks of a long ridge that ran north and south with a crown of piñon and rimrock before him, he took to the road that climbed the face of Red Hill. He chuckled as he saw the red dirt and rocky escarpments, thinking the old-timers did not have to use their imagination to name this Red Hill. The road angled up the face of the long ridge, cut through some of the piñon and over a saddle to overlook the long vista of a vast valley that lay between two long ridges and waved tall prairie grasses like the waves of a sea. He reined up, leaned on his pommel to take in the amazing view, feeling very small and insignificant in such a vast land. Far in the distance, like ripples in the water, mountains stood as shadows in the distance as if marking the boundary of such magnificence. A ribbon of green marked the lowland as a stream danced and twisted its way across the valley floor, robed in willows, alders and chokecherry bushes. It was fertile land and untouched, and Cord shook his head in wonder as he remembered his home in the fertile valley of Missouri where every bit of flatland, especially flat land with ample water, was dotted with farmhouses and fences. But this was nothing but endless grassland, and the only living thing he could see was a distant herd of buffalo showing as dark spots on a canvas of pale tan and dusty green.

He nudged Kwitcher forward, pulling taut the lead line of the mule and following a scampering tail-wagging Blue, his faithful but always curious and exploring hound dog. The road cut through a saddle crossing, angled across the face of the ridge, and pointed east across the head of the valley, hugging a low-rising butte that crowned the north end of the valley. Trout Creek was fed from the high mountains to the north, and bent around the butte on Cord's left. He turned Kwitcher north to follow the creek a short distance as the sun was tucking itself behind the western mountains. A little over a mile brought him to the back side of the butte and a good stand of timber set back from the creek. Cord took a deep breath of the mountain air, knowing they were close to 10,000 feet elevation and although that was a far cry from the 13,000 feet of Mosquito Pass, it was still high country and as the sun lowered, so did the temperature. He moved into the edge of the trees, saw a well-covered site with thickets of juniper and piñon with ample grasses nearby and close enough to the creek. He turned off the roadway, nudging Kwitcher into the shallow creek and rode up the stream before moving across the grassy bank to the timber, reined up to start making his camp. He picketed the horse and mule, and with rifle and binoculars in hand, climbed to the crest of the knoll to get a look at his backtrail.

He bellied down, slipping under the branches of a juniper, and lifted his binoculars to scan the road. A quick look showed nothing on the road across the valley, but movement at the edge of the trees where the road came from Red Hill caught his attention. He watched carefully and spotted the three horses stopped. One of the riders held binoculars and was looking his direction. Cord instantly dropped his glasses, afraid the setting sun might reflect off the lenses and warn the three, but they showed no sign of recognition, and he lifted his binoculars again, watched as they gesticulated, and started moving again, but left the road and moved along the edge of the trees before disappearing beyond his sight, his view obscured by the close-up butte that stood between them.

From his vantage point, Cord looked around the area, saw the flanks of the nearby ridge covered with aspen, the crests showing dark timber, and thought that might be a more appealing camp, but he was satisfied with his own. He was away from the road, near water, had good tree cover, and high ground advantage over any approach. He walked back to his camp, gathering up long dead and dry branches for firewood, knowing he would have only a small hat-sized fire for coffee and to heat up the biscuits and strips of smoked meat, then put it out, and maybe even move his camp away from its present location.

————

HE WAS on the trail before first light, moving across the creek and taking a low cut between two buttes to cross the flats before reaching the road. With the stage road pointing to the northeast and the sun rising slowly behind the eastern mountains, stretching long shadows behind them, he was anxious to put some distance between him and the three riders behind, although they might not be interested in him, but in this land and this time, a man could not be too careful. Often checking his back trail whenever a hill or rise offered a better view, he did not see any sign of riders, thinking they must have turned off or had some other place in mind.

He passed through the sleepy settlement of Como that lay in the shadow of a hillside flanked by a good stand of aspen. Como was nothing more than a typical gold rush-built town with one hotel, one café, a mercantile, and a stage stop. A livery stood on the north end of town with a corral and barn, scattered cabins fringed the settlement and a couple homes showed the promise of a town. But Cord saw one sleepy dog snoozing on the boardwalk that did not even lift his head as they passed, the mercantile owner was shaking a rug off the boardwalk, and gave Cord a nod as he turned back to the door. A stage stood idle but the horses were fresh and the door to the station stood open as the driver came onto the boardwalk, glanced at Cord, then climbed aboard. Cord paid little attention to the activity, but did notice a couple of passengers, both men, come from the station to climb aboard. No one else showed as he rode through the little town.

He felt like a lone sailor on a vast ocean as the grassland stretched beyond his view to the east to touch the hems of the distant blue mountains. Directly east rose a cavalcade of hills with scattered timber on their crests as they marched to the north and their larger hills and distant peaks. Before him stood timber-covered hills and peaks with taller granite-tipped peaks beyond. The stage road took to the shoulders of the hills, crossing the talus slope to round a point into the deeper timber. But that lay in the distance and he guessed it to be at least another five miles and after crossing Tarryall Creek. He would stop for his mid-day break before then and a green ribbon crossed from northwest to southeast and offered water and more. He would learn later that the creek was known as Jefferson Creek, but for now it beckoned both him and the animals and the thick willows and scraggly cottonwoods, offered enough cover for him to have his coffee and give the animals a short rest.

A glance over his shoulder showed the dust cloud of the approaching stage and he readily moved off the road to take cover in the willows before they neared. He was ducking into the brush when a quick glance caught the sight of three riders following after the stage. They paid no attention to Cord and stayed on the trail of the stage, just keeping out of the dust, but staying close. Cord frowned, thinking those were probably the same riders that had been on his back trail, but maybe they were not trailing him. He shrugged and gathered enough twigs and more to make his coffee fire.

He thought about those followers of the stage, wondered if they were up to no good and cut short his nooning. He swung back aboard Kwitcher and took to the road to follow. The hills to the northeast showed the face of the nearest foothills scarred by the slash of the stage road and the stage was just approaching what would be a good climb for already tired horses. As Cord saw the stage start its climb, he saw the three riders taking a narrow trail that took to a saddle between the nearest buttes and what Cord assumed would be a short cut that would probably join the stage road as it bent around the shoulder and into the hills.

Cord shook his head, his suspicions gaining ground and he nudged Kwitcher to a quick walk, and then to a canter. As he neared the cut-off trail, the long-legged grulla stallion stretched out and began the climb of the narrow trail, following the tracks of the three riders. As he neared the crest of the hill, Cord slowed Kwitcher and slowly approached the crest, watching for the riders. The north slope of the hills was thick with timber, but the flanks of the hill leveled out and the stage road was visible below. Cord frowned as he stepped down to look at the tracks of the three and saw where they split up, and started through the timber to make their way down to the road.

Cord knew it was common for stage drivers to stop after a climb to give the horses a blow, and often to allow the passengers to make a quick trip to the bushes. If the three riders were going to rob the stage, that would be the best time. Cord stepped back aboard Kwitcher, started into the timber on the trail of one of the three. It was no more than a half-mile to the road and when he neared, Cord paused, looking through the timber to see the stopped stage and the driver and messenger with their hands up. With Kwitcher ground-tied and the mule's lead line around the saddle horn, Cord stepped down, slipped the Winchester from the scabbard, checked the load, slipped his Colt from the holster and checked its load, reholstered the Colt and started through the timber, using the carpet of pine needles to quiet his approach.

The pines gave way to the thick growth of aspen. The white-barked quakies fluttered in the breeze as Cord picked his way closer. He chose one of the bigger aspen and stood behind the trunk, his body mostly obscured from the outlaws view by the trees and the steep slope that gave him a good view looking down on the drama. He could plainly see the stage and those around it. Two of the riders were on the near side of the coach, one on the far side of the team, facing the driver and messenger. Cord could not make out the words that came from the masked faces but the passengers had already exited the stage and were standing beside the Overland coach, hands raised. Three men all attired like city slickers, one woman and a child, eyes wide with fear. The outlaws were brandishing handguns and barking orders. Cord watched as the driver bent to retrieve the strongbox from the forward boot. It was heavy and the driver asked the messenger's help as they both bent to grab the box. As they came up, the messenger had a shotgun coach gun in his hand and dropped the hammers, blasting the nearest man from his saddle, but he received several bullets from the two on the near side for his trouble. As the messenger slumped in the seat, the frightened driver stammered and struggled with the strongbox. As he pulled it up and rested it on the edge, the outlaw's attention was focused on the box, and Cord used that moment to step closer.

He was near the edge of the trees when he stopped and spoke, "Now it's your turn! Drop those pistols!" he ordered.

Everyone's attention was arrested by the newcomer to the drama and the two riders quickly turned, snapped off a couple shots but the bullets from Cord's Winchester were already on their way and blossomed red on the chest of the nearest outlaw, spun the second outlaw sideways as the bullet tore through his shoulder. The first man dropped his pistol, grabbing at his chest and bending to look. He lifted his eyes back to Cord, down to his chest and slowly closed his eyes as he slid from his saddle. His horse spooked and jumped away to stand and turn to look back at the man who had been his rider.

The second man turned back to face Cord and lifted his pistol to fire, but the Winchester roared again, and the man was driven from his saddle, the bullet tearing into his throat and out the back of his neck. It was in a shower of blood that the man fell into the dirt, rolled over on his face, and lay still in death. The booms of the gunfire had echoed across the narrow draw, causing the six-up to jerk with each blast, but the driver kept them still. The passengers and the driver looked around, seeing each of the outlaws on the ground and then up to see Cord walking from the trees, his Winchester at his side and a sober expression on his face.

"Everybody alright?" he asked, glancing from the passengers to the driver and back to the passengers.

The woman was holding her child, a boy of about six or seven, tight beside her, almost smothering him with his face in the bodice of her dress. She forced a smile and a nod, looking at the other passengers, one of whom was shaking where he stood, nervous hands unbuttoning his vest and collar.

"I think we are, thanks to you, mister," answered the driver, "but I need help with the messenger," nodding to his companion.

25

TRAVEL

"I'd sure feel a lot better if'n you would, friend. What with losin' Abe, our messenger, we ain't got no protection. The stage goes all the way to Denver City and we might be able to get us a shotgunner at one o' the stations, but..." he shrugged, giving Cord a pitiful plea of a look. When Cord did not immediately answer, "You can trail your animals b'hind the coach, an' put your saddle an' packs up top to save 'em a little." He motioned to the top rack of the coach that held just one bag and one small box.

Cord thought about it a moment, he had gone into the woods to get the animals and brought them to the road as the driver was being helped by the passengers to wrap his messenger's body in a canvas to put him up top. They were about ready to leave when Cord rode Kwitcher onto the road, leading the mule and with Blue alongside. He sat in his saddle as he listened to the plea of the driver, glanced to the passengers that waited beside the coach.

When he glanced to the woman, she clasped her hands and added, "Please, mister, I don't know what would have happened if you hadn't come along and I would hate for something like that to happen again." Her little boy was hugging close to her leg and sneaking a look at Cord.

Cord looked at the driver, "How far to your next station?"

"Less'n ten miles. We'll overnight there, the road's too rugged to travel after dark."

"Well, I'll ride along that far," answered Cord, swinging down to strip the gear from the animals.

The driver looked at the dog, glanced to Cord, "We can even put your dog up top, if'n you want."

Cord grinned, slapped his leg and motioned for Blue who came to his side, jumped into his arms, almost knocking him down, and Cord handed him up to the driver for him to ride up top.

"Ahhh, I wanted him to ride inside with me!" declared the previously very quiet little boy looking from Cord to his mother.

Cord grinned, looked at the boy and went to one knee to be on the level with the boy, "Well, young man, Blue can be a handful sometimes and it's best for him to ride out in the open, you know, fresh air and all. Maybe when we get to the stage station, we'll have a chance to get better acquainted. Would that be alright?" asked Cord, focusing all his attention on the boy.

The woman smiled, looked at Cord and said, "This is Jonathan, and you're...?"

Cord smiled, reached out to shake hands with the

boy, and answered, "Pleased to meet you, Jonathan. My name's Cordell Beckett, but most folks call me Cord." He looked up at the boy's mother, a question in his eyes.

"And I'm Meredith, Meredith Willoughby. Pleased to meet you, Mr. Beckett."

Cord let a slow smile split his face as he stood to face the woman, slowly extending his hand to shake. She accepted his hand, smiled and turned back to the stage to load up for the journey.

Cord sat beside the driver, his coach gun in hand and the Winchester in the boot, but within easy reach. He enjoyed the time to look over the country, noticing the south-facing slopes were rather bare save for rocky escarpments, scattered juniper, and lots of rocks and low-growing grass. But the north-facing slopes were heavy with black timber made up of spruce, fir, and ponderosa pine. The road sided Hoosier Creek until the confluence of Hoosier and Kenosha Creek, the latter siding the road to cut its way eastward. With the setting sun at their back, the shadows stretched alongside the road and the air began to turn cool when the driver looked at Cord as he hunkered down in his duster, "Gets a little cool when the sun goes down. We're a little over nine thousand feet along here," he nodded to the distant mountains, "all those peaks do their best to reach fourteen thousand. That's why there's still snow showin' up thar."

"What's the name of the next station?" asked Cord, appreciating the way the driver handled his team.

"They been callin' it Grant station. Ain't much, the station building, couple rooms, a barn for the horses and the corral."

"Is the stage stopping there for the night?" asked Cord, frowning, thinking of the woman and boy and the sleeping arrangements.

"Yup, an' I know what'chur thinkin'. Ever'body just rolls out the blankets on the floor and keeps to themselves. Usually, when we have a woman or so, sometimes they get the back room and the station keeper goes to the barn. We'll just hafta see what kinda mood the ol' boys' in!" he chuckled.

Dusk had lowered its curtain when the stage rolled into the Grant station. The station keeper and his helper unhooked the team and led the horses into the barn for a rub down, while the driver directed the folks to the outhouses and the station. "Ol' George is a purty good cook. His dinners are usually purty good. So, go on in and make yourselves to home an' we'll be in to serve y'all in a little bit."

Cord dropped his gear from the stage, planning on sleeping in the barn with the gear and maybe making an early start well before break of day. It took several trips from the stage with his gear in hand but he soon had his bedroll stretched out in an empty stall, his gear stacked at the head and with his saddle as a pillow. The bags of gold were in opposite panniers for balance, and both panniers were loaded with additional items atop the gold for cover and Cord made certain they were secure and buried under the rest of the gear, two parfleches, extra blankets and canvas cover for the packs, and more. Satisfied with the stall and the arrangement, he followed the driver to the station for some supper.

And the station keeper was determined to live up to the driver's praise. He had prepared a beef and potato and carrot stew that was smelling very good and made Cord's mouth water with hunger. Cord asked about where he got the beef and the station keeper said, "The Meyer Ranch down past Bradford Junction. It's been there a few years an' got a good herd of beef. The stage line pays for it, so we enjoy it!" he chuckled, making short work of serving. Everyone else was gathered around the table, but Cord chose to take his bowl of stew and thick slice of sourdough bread outside, planning on enjoying the last of the sunset and the cool air of the evening while sitting on the bench just outside the door.

He sat down, leaned back against the logs of the station wall, and lifted the bowl just as Meredith and Jonathan came out. She smiled and asked, "May we join you?"

Cord stood, nodding, "Of course, and welcome."

The bench was solid and sizable with ample room for the three with Jonathan in the middle and Blue at Cord's feet, hopeful of leftovers.

Jonathan said, "I like your dog," looking from Blue to Cord.

"Well, he's friendly enough, but he's also protective. I've had him a long time and he's only friendly when he knows I'm comfortable with others."

"Now Jonathan, you finish your supper before you go pettin' the dog," instructed the boy's mother with a sidelong glance to her son and Cord. She looked at Cord, "So, Mr. Beckett, do you just ride around the hills or are you a prospector or...?" she asked as she took a petite bite of the stew.

"Oh, a little of both, ma'am. I'm new to this country

and I like to look around, you know, learn about the country before I make any big decisions. I have done a little prospecting, but nothing serious."

"So, you've no family?"

"No ma'am, you?"

Meredith dropped her eyes and took a deep breath, glanced to Cord and sat her bowl down beside her. "No. My husband was killed working for the Union Pacific Railroad. We are going back to Denver City after visiting my sister in Fairplay. She and her husband have a hotel and store there."

"Do you have other family in Denver City?"

"I have an aunt and her husband that are in business in Denver City. We live and work with them."

"Business?" asked Cord.

"Banking. My aunt's husband is David Moffat, he's the cashier of the First National Bank."

They continued visiting for a little while until Meredith insisted it was time for Jonathan to go to bed. She rose, looked at Cord and said, "It's been nice visiting with you, Mr. Beckett."

"And you, Mrs. Willoughby. Perhaps we'll see one another again sometime."

"Oh, you're not continuing to Denver with the stage?"

"Oh, I think the stage will be fine without me. My horse and dog are anxious to travel alone, that's our way."

Meredith slowly nodded her head, wondering about this unusual man, but asked no more questions and with a nod, turned away and entered the station. Cord slapped his leg for Blue to side him and they walked to the barn to get some sleep before an early start. Cord preferred to set no pattern, do nothing that would cause any suspicion, and avoid as much company as possible. He was still a little nervous about the gold he was carrying.

26

BAILEY'S RANCH

A LITTLE AFTER MIDNIGHT AND CORD ROLLED FROM HIS blankets and saddled Kwitcher, rigged the mule with his packs, and with Blue at his side, rode from the barn. A glance to the moon showed it to be waning from full, but it was a clear night and the brightness of the moon offered ample sight for their travel. The preacher had told him about a trail about four miles east of Grant that cut north from the stage road and would take him over the east shoulder of Mount Logan and drop into the valley of Deer Creek.

"You'll recognize the valley as it's the only one with enough flat land beside it to grow much grass. That valley will take you east and you can get back on the stage road, if'n you're of a mind to, that's what I usually do when I'm goin' thataway." Cord chuckled at the memory of the preacher's deep voice as he related the tales of the trail for him.

Cord had considered the alternate route, knowing it would keep him off the more traveled road and offer solitary travel, however the preacher said it would be slower going and rougher country. By doing much of his travel at night, he would avoid the stages and freighters and others, and have easier going and make better time. He opted for the easier going and kept Kwitcher on the stage road, but with his rifle across the pommel and his duster open to give easy access to his weapons.

As he traveled the lonely road, his mind began to wander back, remembering the woman and the boy on the stage, Meredith and Jonathan. He frowned as he thought how her nearness had reminded him of Yellow Singing Bird, the woman he grew close to after helping her flee her captors and going with her to her people, the Capute Ute in southern Colorado Territory. She in turn left her people to be with him and he was thinking about her becoming his wife when they were attacked and she was killed by the outlaws from the Jayhawkers or Red Legs. The two women were nothing alike, Bird a native woman with long black braids and always attired in buckskin, and Meredith wearing the fashionable attire of the city woman and with a fair complexion and blonde hair. But it was their manner, confidence, and beauty that was shared. He had tried to put Bird from his mind, but all too often her image would come alive before him, or he would hear her voice, or see some mannerism in others that would bring her back.

He shook his head to try to clear his mind and looked at the star-filled sky. There were clouds forming in the east, blocking out the stars and the breeze was cool and smelled of rain. Although he had little experience with the gulley-washers of the mountains, he had heard stories and did not want to be caught in a flash flood. The sun was slowly announcing the new day as it painted the eastern sky in bold strokes of color, making shadows of the distant mountains and making the black timber on Cord's right appear as a thick blanket of darkness, and the scattered juniper and spruce on the left stretch dim shadows across the face of the hillsides. But the rising sun showed itself behind dark clouds, piercing the shrouds with thin lances of light that compounded the threat of a coming storm.

As crooked shafts of lightning began to come from the dark clouds and thunder rumbled over the mountains, Cord approached the stage station known as Bailey's Ranch. The station had the making of a town with the building and barn of the station and an adjoining two-story hotel with a restaurant. Cord stopped at the station, saw the early riser feeding the horses and asked if he could put his animals and gear in a stall while he stopped for breakfast. "Shore, that'd be alright. 'Course I might put you to work to earn their keep!"

"Soon's I get some breakfast in me I just might do that!" grinned Cord, stepping down to lead Kwitcher and the mule into the barn. He stripped their gear, stacked it in the stall, covering the panniers with his saddle and blanket, gave the animals a quick rubdown and a fork full of hay, then walked to the restaurant for his breakfast.

He stepped into the big room to be greeted by a woman that showed grey in her hair and a smile on her face. She wiped her hands on her apron, motioned for Cord to have a seat at a table and came to stand beside him, "We got bacon n' eggs, biscuits n' gravy, steak an' taters, what's your pleasure?"

Cord smiled, "Sounds good. I'll have some."

The woman frowned, "Some what?"

"What you just said."

A slow smile split the woman's face, "I like a man with an' appetite!" and turned on her heel to march to the kitchen. Cord had barely settled into his chair with a view of the roadway when she returned with a tin cup and a pot of steaming coffee. She poured a cup and marched back to the kitchen. When she returned, she had an armful of plates and a smile almost as big. She sat the plates down in a semi-circle before Cord and stood back with hands on hips, "Now, let's see you do sumpin' with all that!" and slapped her hands together and spun around and marched off with her hips bouncing and making Cord think of two pigs in a poke fighting to get out.

He enjoyed the meal, and with empty plates before him, he sat back, patted his belly and smiled as the woman returned to clean off the table. She stood, hands on hips, smiling broadly, "You done it! I din't think you could, but you done it, shore 'nuff!" and bent to pick up the plates. She paused, looked at Cord, and in a soft voice, "Don't suppose you'd want a piece of fresh pecan pie for dessert."

"No, ma'am, I'm plumb full. However, if'n you could wrap it up, the whole pie maybe, I'd be might pleased to take it with me!" grinned Cord.

The woman smiled, nodded, and marched off to the kitchen, hands full and humming a happy tune. She returned just as a clap of thunder rattled the windows, and a bolt of lightning split a big spruce across the road. The woman jumped, the pie flew up in the air and Cord jumped to catch it, and with it clasped firmly in his hands, he sat back down and gingerly sat the pie package before him. The woman stood wide-eyed, glancing from Cord to the window and back again. "You might be stuck in here a while."

"Nope, I've got to tend to my animals in the barn, maybe help the hostler."

"Then you be careful, an' I hope to see you again," she nodded sternly, picked up the coin Cord had placed on the table to pay, and returned to the kitchen. Cord rose, walked to the door and as the rain came with a roar and a rattle of windows and more, he turned up the collar of his duster, pulled his hat down tight, and with the pie package under an arm, he left the restaurant at a fast walk and went to the barn of the station. When he stepped into the barn, he stopped, shook off the excess and started to the stall where his animals were tethered and was greeted by a wagging and smiling Blue. He placed the pie package atop his gear, frowned as he looked about, and thought something was wrong. Somebody had been in his gear. He turned around, looking about the barn, but no one was in the building. He bent to look through his gear, especially the panniers where the gold was stashed and began digging into each one to check the bags of gold. Nothing was missing, although it was evident someone had been searching through the packs and more.

The rain appeared to be letting up a mite when Cord heard the rattle of trace chains and the rumble and splash of the stage and team. The driver pulled the stage as close to the barn as possible and hollered for the hostler, "Hey Tater! Where's muh horses?!" but there was no response. Cord looked around, waiting to see the hostler called Tater to show, but no one moved.

The driver climbed down as Cord walked to the big barn door that stood wide open and the driver was surprised to see him. "Well howdy, Cord! I wondered what happened to you since you were gone from Grant! What'chu doin' here?"

"Oh, just stopped for breakfast an' the rain came, so..." he shrugged.

"You seen the hostler?" asked the driver.

"Not since I first came in here, earlier." He looked at the driver, "Say, I never did get your name."

The man grinned, extended his hand, "I'm called Woody, muh names Wilson Wood."

"Alright Woody, I reckon it's up to us to get you fresh horses. I'll see if'n I can round up a team while you unhitch them," stated Cord, nodding to the wet horses as he turned to go deeper into the barn.

"Wait a' bit, Cord. What with this rain an' such, we'll probably hafta wait a while for the road to dry out a spell. Ain't no way I'm climbin' that hill in the mud. We probably won't leave till after noon, dependin'."

"Well, I'll probably be gone by then, and you'll find the hostler. So," he extended his hand, "It's been good to know you, Woody. Maybe we'll meet up again someday."

"Maybe. Yuh never know," agreed Woody, smiling and shaking Cord's hand.

He turned away, stepped into the rain to tell the passengers about their layover, giving them the choice of staying in the mostly dry coach, or going to the restaurant for a meal. The rain had let up some and they all made the choice of a meal. When they came from the coach, Meredith happened to glance Cord's way, smiled and turned away to go to the restaurant.

Cord had a thought of going to the restaurant again, but he did not want to leave his gear unattended and wanted to get ready to leave. He shook his head, mumbling to himself something about being a fool and began gearing up his animals.

27

BETRAYAL

CORD DID NOT LIKE THE IDEA OF TRAVELING THE STAGE ROAD after someone had searched his packs, but for the route, it was the easiest and fastest way to make time toward Denver City. When he left Bailey's Ranch, it was pushing toward mid-morning and according to the two-dollar pocket watch that hung on a chain at Cord's belt, it was just shy of ten O'clock. The rain had lessened to little more than a drizzle, but the road would be a muddy problem for the stage and team. He kept to the shoulder of the road where there was grass and more that made for better footing, and started the climb into the hills from Bailey's. It was a steady climb but not steep enough to cause difficulty for Kwitcher or the mule. After just over a mile, it leveled out a short distance and began another climb for just under a mile. After cresting the second rise, the road began its twisting journey through the timber-covered hills and on both sides of the road, the conifer forest of ponderosa, fir, and spruce stood tall and unyielding against the morning rain.

The storm lessened and the sun began to show itself just after mid-day and the slight breeze aided the drying out of the road and the rider as well as the animals. Even Blue was in better spirits and began his usual lead-the-way runaway to scout the trail before them. After the crest of the second climb, the road took them across Deer Creek and over a slight rise before turning to the south across the face of a rocky-topped hill and then back to the northeast to crest a bit of a saddle where Cord reined up as Blue came from the trees. He looked at the dog, knew there was something he didn't like as he came beside Cord and Kwitcher, turned to look back at the trees on the south side of the road, teeth showing and a low growl rising. Cord slipped the Winchester to set the butt on his thigh, a round in the chamber and the hammer cocked. With his finger on the trigger, he held the rifle on his thigh and nudged Kwitcher forward.

They came from the trees, neckerchiefs covering their faces, they came from the uphill side which was to Cord's advantage as he held the rifle, lowered it across the pommel and with the muzzle in their direction, he watched as the men came forward. He recognized the clothing and stature of the man on the right as the hostler from the stage station, the one Woody had called Tater.

It was Tater who spoke, "We'll be takin' that thar mule an' those packs!"

Cord did not respond but watched as the man to the left nudged his mount around behind the mule, apparently planning on taking the lead from Cord. But Cord knew his mule and what he would do, for the animal did not like anything behind him and when

Cord jerked the lead, the big mule humped his back and kicked back with both hind feet, knocking the horse staggering and the rider fighting to stay aboard, but neither managed to keep their place as the horse fell, kicking as he did and the rider was unseated, screaming, "Muh legs busted! That mule broke it!" He was reaching toward his bent leg as he tried to pull the other one from under his horse.

The ruckus had surprised the other two outlaws and Cord dropped the hammer on the one called Tater, the blast from the Winchester echoing across the flats and bouncing from the rocky slope. The bullet drove Tater from his saddle and spooked his horse that lifted his tail and dropped his head as he bucked away through the timber.

Cord instantly jacked another round into the Winchester, brought it to bear on a wide-eyed outlaw who stammered and cried, "No, mister! Don't shoot!" and tossed his pistol aside as he lifted his hands and whimpered, "I don' wanna die!"

"Then you best be for gatherin' up this mess and givin' up on bein' an outlaw. All it'll getchu is killed! But first, answer me this, why'd you come after me?"

"Uh, uh, Tater there said you had a bag o' gold in yore packs. Said you'd be an easy take."

"He was wrong on both counts," growled Cord, nudging Kwitcher into a canter to put some distance behind them, giving the trembling would-be outlaw only a glance. The mule stayed close on his heels and Blue, happy again, led the way. He thought to himself, *"Prob'ly shoulda killed the other two, but..."* he shook his head, thinking about both his father and the preacher and what they would have to say about all the killing he had done since he left the farm. He didn't like killing, but he was pretty sure he'd like dying even less. He also thought that was his own fault for letting the bags out of his sight when he went to breakfast. He knew he was getting close to Denver but thought he would have to spend at least one more night on the trail and wherever that was, he was going to use those packs for a pillow and not let them out of his sight again.

He rode a few miles past Bradford Junction with it stage station, hotel, and store, and after dusk lowered its curtain and he was riding with the dim light of sundown at his back, he left the road and took a little-used trail into a cut between a couple buttes, found a good spot in the black timber with a little clearing and made camp for the night. Rising again well before first light, he was on the road in the silence of the dim light before dawn, enjoying the peacefulness and quiet, until a pair of freighters rounded a bend before him, each big wagon drawn by four pair of plodding oxen and driven by two teamsters. Without a nod or a wave, the teamsters kept their wagons in the middle of the road, forcing Cord and his animals to the side. Once past, Cord continued but had gone just a short ways when he saw a crew of workers using teams of Percherons pulling scrapers, wagons and more as the crew was busy working on the road, both widening and smoothing and more. He reined up next to a man standing and watching and asked, "What's that all about?"

The man chuckled, removed the big pipe from his mouth and said, "Why, boy, those men are building a road! Cain'tchu tell?"

"But there's already a road here," answered Cord,

pushing his hat back from his brow and leaning on the pommel.

"Ah, but it's gonna be a better road, wide 'nuff for wagons to pass each other an' better grade an' more. It's called the Bradford Toll Road."

"Toll road? You mean they're gonna charge folks to use it?"

"That's right. How else they gonna pay for it?"

Cord shook his head, "If'n that don't beat all. Next they'll be chargin' for the air we breathe!" he grumbled, nudging Kwitcher forward, "C'mon boy, we need to get to town 'fore they start askin' fer money!"

It was late in the afternoon when he rounded a bend and looked at the distant flats to the east. Before him marched a line of hog-back ridges acting like a fence to keep the mountains from rushing out onto the plains. In a break between the hogbacks, Cord could see the buildings of Denver City and knew he was within reach of the big city, but it was getting late in the day, and he wanted to have ample time to go to the bank, and hopefully see Dave Cook and maybe others as Cracker had advised. He moved away from the road to a bit of a draw below a rock outcropping that appeared as a stack of dominoes lying at an angle and stuck in the side of the hill. In the bottom of the draw, a little creek chuckled beneath the junipers and piñons and offered Cord a decent campsite well away from the road, but just to be safe, he picked his way across the rocks, and would not make a fire this night.

Although his camp was out of sight of the road, around a point of rocks and hidden in the trees, Cord did not sleep well. There were travelers passing going both ways until well after dark. He heard the stage come over the hill and head to town, heard more freighters, maybe the same ones coming back empty, and other wagons and more. He shook his head as he lay in his blankets, hands behind his head, staring at the darkening sky as the stars lit their lanterns for the night.

As was his habit, he was up well before first light, spent some time in prayer and reading, wanting to re-establish his habit of mornings with his Lord, and making a hat-sized fire for some coffee, he was refreshed and ready by the time the sun peeked over the eastern horizon. He rode with the sun in his eyes as he followed the road into Denver City. He split the hogbacks, crossed Bear Creek at Pennsylvania Crossing, and followed a rough road toward the city. He crossed the Platte River on a low wooden bridge and took another road that pointed to the heart of the city.

He saw an old gentleman sitting on his porch in a rocking chair and watching the doin's of the morning and Cord reined up, called out, "Excuse me, sir. Can you tell me how to find the First National Bank?"

"Hehehehe...gonna rob it, are ya?"

Cord chuckled, "Nope, I was told to see a fella there, 'bout a business of some sort. Ain't never been to the big city 'fore, so don't know much 'bout it."

"Wal, it's easy to find. That road yore on thar'," he pointed with his pipe stem, and looked to his right, "will take you into town. Find a street called 15th Street and turn to yore right an' you'll see a kinda new, two-story brick building with arches o'er the windows. That'll be the bank. They're the only ones can afford foolishness like arches an' such!" grumbled the old man.

Cord nodded, waved, "Thank you sir! I greatly appreciate the help!" and nudged Kwitcher onward.

_____

28

BUSINESS

CORD SPOTTED THE BUILDING AND REINED UP IN FRONT. HE looked around, but there were no hitchrails, just posts with rings and he was a little confused, but he saw a buggy stop and the driver step out, take a line from the horse's bridle and tie it to the ring on the post and step up on the boardwalk and Cord chuckled, stepped down and tethered Kwitcher, tugged on the lead rope of the mule and tied him off as well. He motioned for Blue to stay with the animals and he lifted the canvas panniers from the packsaddle, carried them like satchels and stepped into the bank.

He stopped, looking around, and a young man at a desk nearby asked, "May I help you?" frowning at Cord and cocking his head to the side to look him over.

Cord grinned, "I need to make a deposit for the mercantile back in Oro City. I was told by Michael Densmore they had an account here and this, nodding to and lifting one of the packs, is the deposit."

The young man frowned, "Is that money?"

Cord shook his head, "Same as."

The young man stood, walked to a nearby door and knocked. Cord noticed the name on the door was David Moffat and Cord remembered Meredith saying that was her aunt's husband. He chuckled to himself, still wondering why she didn't just say he was her uncle. But the young man had disappeared into the office, soon returned and motioned for Cord to come into the room. He pushed past the young man, set the bags down, and looked at David Moffat. He was an austere man, bald on top with hair above his ears on both sides, a handlebar moustache, and somewhat portly but appeared to be pretty stout. He stood, and with a stoic expression extended his hand, "I'm David Moffat and you're...?"

"I'm Cordell Beckett," answered Cord, shaking hands with the man as the banker looked at Cord and his attire with a rather judgmental expression, but Cord grinned, "and I've got a little deposit for your bank from the mercantile in Oro City, and Michael Densmore."

"I'm familiar with Mr. Densmore," responded the man, looking at the bags, "and the deposit?"

"You'll need some scales. There's a bit of dust there, 'bout a hundred pounds," answered Cord, glancing to see the change of expressions on the man who stepped back, looking from Cord to the bags, and motioning to the clerk to fetch the scales. When the young man returned, there was another clerk with him and they set up the scales on a narrow table that rested against the wall and turned as Cord lifted the first bag from the pannier. They poured out the dust into a larger bowl-like container with a bit of a spout and fingered the dust, their eyes growing larger as they did. When they looked at Moffat and nodded, the banker smiled and said, "Well, that *is* quite a deposit. We'll measure it out and tally it up for you. It might take a little while."

Cord chuckled, "I've got time, but while they're doing that, could you tell me where I might find Dave Cook, the man that was a federal marshal?"

The banker sat down, locked his fingers across his paunch and glared at Cord, "And what is your business with Mr. Cook?"

"Oh, and I'd also like to find the headquarters for the Colorado Rangers, if they have one," ignoring the banker's inquiry.

"Tell me, Mr. Beckett, is it? Tell me, did you bring this all the way from Oro City alone?" asked the banker, frowning.

"I did," replied a grinning Cord.

"Wasn't that rather foolish?"

"Why?"

"Well, there are all sorts of highwaymen that would like to relieve you of such a sum."

"If they knew, but..." he shrugged. "There were a few that tried, but as you see..." he motioned to the bags.

"Are you connected with the Rangers?"

"No," answered Cord, offering nothing additional. He frowned, then looked to the banker, "Are you the David Moffat that has a niece by the name of Meredith Willoughby?"

The banker sat up, "How do you know Meredith?"

"Oh, I don't *know* her, but I did meet her and the boy at one of the stage stops. They were on their way here, might have already made it."

At that moment, there was a knock at the door and

it opened without waiting and in stepped a very pretty Meredith, smiling broadly as she stepped around Cord, "Uncle David, I'm back!" and gave the big man an affectionate hug. She turned and recognized Cord, "Why, Mr. Beckett, I certainly did not expect to see you here."

Cord stood, removed his hat, and nodded, "Mrs. Willoughby, pleased to see you again. How's Jonathan?"

She smiled, dropped her eyes, "Oh he's fine, a little tired from the trip, but you know, boys will be boys and recuperate in short order." She motioned for him and her uncle to sit down.

"Yes ma'am," responded Cord as he seated himself, running his fingers through his tousled hair, appearing a little embarrassed.

Meredith looked at her uncle, "You said something about a job?"

"We'll talk about it later, Meredith. I'll come to the house for lunch and we can talk then." His tone was dismissive and she nodded, backed away and turned to leave but before leaving, she looked at her uncle, "Oh, you might want to know, Mr. Beckett saved the lives of Jonathan, myself, and everyone else on the stage. He's quite a man." She turned to the door, cast a smile to Cord and exited the office. Cord looked at the banker, saw his expression of disapproval and turned to look at the clerks weighing the gold dust.

It took them a good while and when they finished, they turned to look at Cord and the banker. The clerk looked at his tally sheet and said, "At today's prices, that comes to $56,789.00."

Cord saw the banker's eyes grow wide and his brow lift at the numbers. He was definitely surprised and pleased. He looked to Cord, "Is that all to be deposited or..."

Cord said, "No, he asked me to bring whatever was over fifty thousand back in currency and coin. But if you don't mind, I've had enough of sleepless nights. I'd like a couple hundred in cash, and I'll come back for the rest before I leave. I'd like to get a good room, get cleaned up, see if I can meet with a couple men, and have a good meal before a night's rest. Could you recommend a good hotel and restaurant?"

"Certainly, certainly. Just around the corner is the Denver House and there is a restaurant there as well. And we'll certainly accommodate you regarding the currency." He looked to the clerk, "Put the dust in the safe and bring Mr. Beckett two hundred dollars in currency and coin, right away!" The clerk nodded, grabbed an armload of bags of dust and with the other clerk on his heels and loaded down as well, the two scurried away to do the banker's bidding.

Cord left the bank with partially empty panniers that still held the rest of his gear he used to cover the gold, strapped them on the mule and untied the animals, walking with them to the office of Dave Cook. He spotted a sign painted on a window, *Denver Marshal Office,* and stopped to tie off the animals. He stepped into the office, looking about and a man at a desk, "May I help you?"

"Is Mr. Cook here?"

"He is in his office. Do you have business with him?"

"I was told to talk to him when I got in town. We have a mutual friend, Cracker Tibbs, down in Oro City, who told me I should talk to him about a legal matter."

"Your name, sir?"

"Cordell Beckett."

The man nodded, stood and walked to a closed door, rapped on the doorframe, and at a word, stepped inside. He returned, motioned for Cord to follow, and escorted him to the office. When Cord stepped in, the man behind the desk stood, grinning, and extended his hand, "So, ol' Cracker told you to come see me. Must be important as that ol' sourdough doesn't often have much to say." After shaking Cord's hand, he motioned him to be seated and he sat as well. "So, what's this *legal matter* all about?"

29

PROPOSITION

THE MAN BEHIND THE DESK HAD ROUND SPECTACLES, A GREY handlebar moustache, dark eyes, sparse eyebrows, and a full head of hair. His face appeared to be frozen in a frown and his eyes were piercing as he visually examined Cord. He leaned forward, forearms on the desktop, as Cord began to tell his tale, beginning with the assault on his homeplace and the murder of his family. Leaving no details untouched, he related all the happenings since and up to include his journey to Denver City.

The big man sat back, frowning as he looked at Cord, judging the validity of the tale he just heard, "And what did you say brought you to Denver City?"

"Cracker and his friend, Mike Densmore, asked me to bring some gold dust to the banker."

"How much?"

"Well, the final tally was just a little over fifty-six thousand dollars," stated Cord with a resolute expression as he looked at Cook.

The man frowned, leaned forward again, "Did you say fifty-six thousand?" he asked, somewhat stunned. When Cord nodded, Cook frowned and stated, "Usually for that amount, it would require at least a wagon guarded by a dozen or so trained men, and you were alone?"

"Yessir."

"Any trouble?"

"Once, but 'tweren't much."

"What exactly was not much?"

"Three men came from the trees, my mule got one, I shot one, the other'n gave up an' I left."

"Why didn't you bring him in?"

"Didn't have any authority, which is why I'm here. Cracker thinks I should have a badge of some kind, and he said you could help with that."

"You still huntin' some o' them Jayhawkers?"

"Ran into some down to Oro City, I think they're plannin' on doin' some raiding of the claims around there and if they succeed, there will be no stopping them. They think nothing of killing first and taking everything."

Cook sat there for a moment, obviously thinking about the request and looking at this man before him. He stood, went to the coat rack in the corner and picked up his hat, turned and looked at Cord, "C'mon with me. There's somebody I want you to meet."

Cord nodded, stood and followed the man from his office. They walked outside and went down the board-walk around the corner and down the street another block. Cook took a couple steps up to enter the double doors of the brick building and once in the lobby of the building, went to a short hallway and rapped on a door, and without awaiting an answer, stepped inside, Cord close beside him. Both men doffed their hats and a man at a desk stood, "Marshal Cook, good to see you. Marshal Shaffenburg is waiting," and motioned for him to go to the inside office. Cook rapped a couple times and at an answer from within, stepped inside, holding the door for Cord. Cook stepped to the desk where a tall, lean man stood smiling and with his hand extended to shake with Cook. "Good to see you again, Dave," he frowned as he looked past Cook to Cord, "And who's this with you?"

Cook turned slightly to Cord, "This is Cordell Beckett, I wanted you to meet him and see if you could help out a little."

Shaffenburg nodded, motioned for them to be seated, and sat down, leaned back and looked from one to the other, waiting for an explanation.

Cook began, "Well M.A., I knew you wanted a report on the Musgrove-Franklin case and I thought to bring this young man along. You see, well, I'll let him tell you his story." He looked to Cord, nodded, and Cord scooted forward on his seat a little and began to relate the same account as given to Cook, about his hunt that began when his family was murdered.

"So you see, sir, I've been after this bunch for quite a while and up to now, I haven't had to have any badge or authority, honestly, I never thought of it. I've been so consumed with vengeance or huntin' justice, whatever you want to call it, I've been a little blinded. But I'm beginning to see the need for a dividing line between a personal vendetta and a need for right versus wrong.

After talking with, or being talked to by, Cracker Tibbs, and then some time with the Reverend Dyer, I believe the right way would be to be on the right side of the law, although I have tried to do that, but it would be best to make it official."

Shaffenburg looked to Dave Cook, "And what makes you think he would make a good marshal? That is what you're thinking, isn't it?"

Cook let a quick grin split his face and he looked from Shaffenburg to Cord, "Well, I know Cracker and Mike Densmore, and they've recommended him pretty highly. You see, they had him carry about a hundred pounds of gold dust from Oro City here to Denver City and put it in the bank."

The federal marshal frowned, looking from Cook to Cord and back to Cook. "A hundred pounds? That's what, over fifty thousand dollars worth? And he brought it by himself?"

"That's right."

The marshal looked at Cord, "So, if I make you a deputy, are you gonna be like Dave here and shoot all your outlaws?" he chuckled as he glanced at Cook.

Cook frowned, "Now hold on! There were two of 'em and I only shot one! Didn't I bring in the leader, Musgrove?"

"Yeah, but you shot Ed Franklin!" chuckled the marshal.

Cord interjected, "Well, to be honest, that's one of the reasons I haven't had to bring anyone in, most of 'em were killed where they were, not that I wanted it that way, but when it was either them or me, I chose them."

Cook chuckled, "Good choice, Cord."

"Well, we could use somebody down there in the middle of gold country. So," he paused, looking at Cord, "If I make you a temporary deputy, will you do more than just chase Jayhawkers?"

"I will. Whatever is needed, I'll do it."

"Alright, then stand and raise your right hand," directed the marshal, as he himself stood. He looked at Cord, began to recite the oath of office, paused as Cord repeated it and finalized with, "alright Mr. Beckett. You go to that man at the desk out front, he'll give you a booklet on the laws and duties and a badge. And you'll be reporting to me and this office. Understand?"

"Yessir," and at the marshal's dismissive wave, Cord exited the office and went to the man at the desk and retrieved the necessary badge and information.

He was about to leave when Cook came out, called to him and asked, "Where you stayin'?"

"I'm at the Denver House."

"I'll stop by later, we'll have dinner and talk," stated Cook, and Cord knew that was not a request but a directive. Cord nodded and exited the building. He wanted to make a stop at a haberdashery and get some new clothes, his were getting a little on the raggedy side.

He had passed a store that looked to be what he wanted and he walked in, looked around and a man came and rubbing his hands together, looked up and down at Cord's clothes and asked, "And how may we help you, sir?"

————

A KNOCK CAME on Cord's hotel room door, and he opened the door to see the front desk clerk standing, "Mr. Beckett?"

"Yes," answered Cord.

"Marshal Cook asked me to tell you he'll be waiting in the dining room for you, sir."

"Oh, good, good. You can tell him I'll be right down."

"Very good sir."

Cord picked through some of his new clothing, opting for his black sack coat over the pinstriped trousers. A white linen shirt, open at the collar and a new black felt hat topped it off and a new pair of black boots with the pants leg on the outside completed the ensemble. He felt good, and his confidence showed. He was a handsome man with his newly trimmed whiskers, he showed a bit of mystery, and his dark eyes missed nothing. When he stepped into the dining room, he spotted the marshal and went directly to his table and had no sooner seated himself than a waiter appeared and offered to take their order.

The marshal said, "We'll start with coffee, please, and we'll look over the menu."

The waiter quickly left to fetch the coffee and the marshal looked at Cord, "I almost didn't recognize you. You clean up pretty well."

Cord grinned, "I don't get the opportunity to do this very often, but it feels good to have had a bath and all. But...I'll be headin' out tomorrow and put the big city far behind me."

"I understand that, but there's something you need to know."

Cord frowned, "Before we get into that, I've been

curious ever since I heard the two of you talking about it, what's this about a fella named Musgrove?"

The marshal grinned, dropped his eyes, and began to explain, "He and a fella named Ed Franklin had a gang of outlaws and murderers, they were credited with at least a dozen murders, all over the state, although I'm not sure they ever made it over to Oro City, but most everywhere else. I tracked 'em down, arrested Musgrove and figured Franklin would try to bust him out, so I kinda laid a trap for him. When he came into town, I heard about it, went to his hotel and he drew his gun, I had to shoot him. That's about it." Cord looked at the man and knew there was probably a lot more to the story, but he was the kind of man that kept things close to his chest, and Cord certainly understood that.

"Now, here's what you need to know." He looked around to see if anyone was close enough or paying extra attention to them, and satisfied, he leaned a little closer to Cord and spoke softly, "Your new boss, Marshal Sheffenburg, has been known to cut a few corners when it comes to what's right and wrong. What I want you to know, is you do not have to follow that example. I think you're a man that wants to do what's right, and that's what I expect of you. Just don't let anything you see or hear about your boss influence you, understood?"

"But won't that affect what I do as a deputy?"

"Not necessarily. Folks will be watching and judging you for who you are and what you do, so just be sure your tracks follow the right trail." Cook looked directly at Cord, then leaned back and glanced around to make certain no one was eavesdropping. He saw the waiter approaching and nodded, waited for him to pour the coffee and asked, "What's the special for tonight?"

"Beef stroganoff with egg noodles."

Cook looked at Cord with raised eyebrows as if asking the question. Cord nodded in return and Cook nodded to the waiter, "We'll have that, thank you."

30

RETURN

CORD WAS ATTIRED MUCH THE SAME, BUT HE HAD HIS whiskers trimmed, a new hat and clothes and his duster was clean, yet he had the saddlebags over his shoulder as he pushed his way into the bank. With a glance to the clerk at the desk, he walked straight to the banker's office, rapped on the door, and with a hail from within, walked into the office. Mr. Moffat stood with his hand extended and a broad smile on his face, "Mr. Beckett, I was expecting you. Please, have a seat."

Cord grinned, shook the banker's hand and seated himself, hanging the saddlebags on the arm of the chair beside him. He chuckled to himself at the change in attitude of the banker from his first visit, but accepted the man's greetings and asked, "You have the cash we discussed?"

"Certainly, certainly," He picked up a large envelope at the side of his desk and withdrew a considerable stack of currency and a handful of coin and began to count it out. When he finished, he looked at Cord, "That's the balance of the amount for the gold, minus the two hundred dollars we already provided to you. Do you agree?"

"Yes sir, that about sums it up," replied Cord as he began placing the cash in the bottom of his saddlebags. He had the bags fashioned with a false bottom in each pouch, enabling him to place about half the amount in each bag, cover it with the leather false bottom, and fill the rest of each bag with personal items.

As Cord filled the bags, the banker asked, "And were you successful in your meetings with the marshal and the Rangers?"

Cord smiled, nodded, mumbled, "Mmmmhummm," and continued filling the bags. He was thinking about his meeting with Ranger Colonel Samuel Tappan and the Colorado Rangers. Marshal Cook had taken him to their office earlier this morning, introduced Cord and made his recommendation that the Rangers make Cord an official Ranger. "Even though he is officially a deputy marshal, the additional authority of the Rangers might carry a little more weight in some areas. And unless I miss my guess, Cord here will be covering considerable territory in his work."

The leader of the Rangers agreed with Cook, adding, "Well, we've been looking for additional men and what with the gold strikes, many of those that would usually be available have chosen to dig in the dirt instead." He nodded to Cord, "We have had an excellent record and because of the Rangers participation in the Battle of Glorieta Pass, we have a reputation of honor and glory that each ranger is expected to uphold, however, I do not think it necessary to make you a ranger, but I will assure you that you have our unconditional support in whatever task you undertake, so, feel free to call upon us at any time." Colonel Tappan nodded to Marshal Cook, extended his hand to Cord and wished him well.

Cord was just finishing stuffing his bags when another rap on the door admitted the pretty Meredith who smiled at Cord, "Why, Mr. Beckett, this is getting to be a habit. And a habit I certainly did not expect, especially for us to meet in my uncle's office."

Cord had stood when Meredith entered, smiled at her remark and replied, "Well, I'm certain this is the last you'll be seeing of me, Mrs. Willoughby, I'm leaving town today and returning to Oro City." Cord looked past the smiling Meredith to see the squirrelly clerk rise from his desk and scurry out the front door, he frowned thinking that was a little odd, but there's no under-standing city folk. He looked back to Meredith, smiled and slung his saddlebags over his shoulder, "So, if you'll excuse me, I need to finish packing my things before I leave town."

He tipped his hat and with a nod and a "thank you" to the banker, he walked from the office, anxious to get back into the mountains and away from so many people.

When he exited the bank, he was surprised to see Marshal Cook standing by the hitching post where Kwitcher and the pack mule were tethered. He nodded to Cord, "Thought I'd see you off. And...there's some news I heard that you might be interested in."

Cord stepped beside Kwitcher and began strapping on his saddlebags and once secure, went to the parfleche to get some of his new clothing to put in the saddlebags atop the cash. Cook began to explain, "There's a Ute chief, Nicaagat, most call him Captain

Jack, he's a compadre of Chief Ouray. He and Ouray
went with Carson to Washington in January as part of a
negotiation for a new treaty. But last I heard, Cap'n Jack
was not too happy about it. Their last treaty gave the
Ute most of the western half of Colorado, from the
107th meridian to the Utah border. But the new treaty
wants to put 'em all on smaller reservations, and many
of 'em don't like it. Among those is Captain Jack and
he's leading an uprising that could take in all of your
territory. I did get a report that some renegades hit a
couple freighters, killed some men and ransacked the
freighters, but that was just the word of some other
travelers. Nothin' official."

"So, what you're saying is I need to watch out for
anything wearing buckskin or sportin' feathers?"
chuckled Cord.

"Well, there's been a bunch of Utes under chief
Colorow that have kept company with the Rooney's at
their ranch beyond the hogbacks, there's a spring near
there they call Iron Spring and the chief an' his leaders
use that for some o' their councils. And they've usually
been friendly, but I'm guessin' some o' their young
warriors have a little blood lust and are wantin' to
prove themselves. And, since you've already traveled
that way and are packin' some money, you probably
need to watch for anything or anyone that you don't
know, and...well, I'd say, don't trust anything wearin'
pants, or...not," replied the marshal, grinning at Cord.

"Well marshal, if you're gettin' bored in the big city,
you can always come south with me for a short visit."

"Oh, I got enough excitement right here. I already
made one trip chasin' outlaws, I think I'll just stay
'round town where there's good eating and soft beds."

"You're gettin' soft, Marshal," chuckled Cord, swinging up on Kwitcher. He glanced down the street, frowned, looked down at the marshal, "See that man down there, leaning on the side of the building and kinda lookin' this way, you know him?"

"No, but I know the type, why?"

"I saw the clerk in the bank talkin' to him right after I came out, before I saw you."

"Be careful, I never did like that squirrelly little sissy britches, and anybody that knows him ain't worth trustin'."

Cord nodded, swung Kwitcher around and with a wave over his shoulder, started out of town. Tired of the stench of the city, he was anxious for the fresh air of the high country, air that was scented with the pungent yet sweet smell of pine and the flutter of aspen leaves. He had become accustomed to the beauty of quakies that often fringed the black timber with snow-capped granite-tipped peaks standing proudly above as they stretched high to scratch the blue of the sky. Although a newcomer to the high country, it had already become a part of Cord, his senses, his being, his identity. Not only did he now have purpose, he had a responsibility and that not just to himself, but to the country, gold country, the high country of Colorado Territory.

He crossed the old wooden bridge that spanned the Platte River, took the stage road that split the hogbacks and climbed into the foothills. Dust hung heavy in the roadway and the wide tracks in the dirt told of freight wagons not too far ahead. The stage road he traveled was already being called the Bradford Road, and when finished, it would become a toll road. Cord had heard talk in the dining room about all the construction going on, and of special interest was the road construction, and the businessmen were discussing how those roads could impact their businesses. "Instead of us waitin' for those gold diggers to come to town to buy their equipment and supplies, there'll be regular freight routes throughout the gold fields. We'll just have to let those mine companies know about what we have to offer," was the conversation that Cord remembered. He shook his head at the thought of big businesses coming into the wild and woolly gold camps, he was certain they had no idea what they would be dealing with, or who. But he had already seen what sudden riches can do to a man and his judgment about what he would spend his money on and how readily he listened to the pitch of some slick-tongued salesman.

The road that climbed out of the valley cut through rough country, high rocky steep-sided hills, and wherever there was enough dirt there was usually a spruce or pine struggling to gain footing enough to grow tall. The many rocky escarpments protruded through the timber and marked every hillside with nature's warning of slide rock and rugged country. The stage road bent and twisted around the flanks and ridges of the hills, ever working higher climbing about a thousand feet in elevation in less than four miles. But it was there that the road dropped into the wide basin that was shielded by the long line of tall hills on the east and turned to the south to start its meandering trek to the southwest always climbing and crossing the many hills and more that would take him into the lap of the high Rockies and South Park, before crossing Mosquito Pass at 13,000 feet or more.

31

RETURN

"I GOT COFFEE ON!" CAME A FAMILIAR VOICE FROM A BREAK IN the trees on the east side of the stage road. Sitting below a rocky escarpment that would better be described as a big chunk of rock that looked like a granite cliff, was a familiar face. Cracker grinned and motioned to Cord to join him. Cord was surprised to see him but eager to talk with his friend and readily reined his grulla into the trees to follow Cracker into his camp on the lee side of the rocks. Cracker walked to his simmering fire, bent to pick up the coffee pot and pour a couple cups. He watched Cord step down, ground tying his horse and the mule, and come close to accept the steaming cup of java. Cracker motioned him to a log and he sat on a big rock, grinning all the while, knowing Cord was as curious as an eager youngster, and began to explain, "I just wanted to see how you was doin', you bein' new to these parts. Thought you might need a little help," he chuckled as he sipped his coffee, the steam rising to mask his eyes.

Cord leaned forward, resting his elbows on his

knees, took a deep sip, and answered, "Doin' alright. No real problems. Met the marshal, he gimme a badge, just goes to show how hard up they are for deputies."

"Well dadgum it! That puts a kink in my garter! We was gonna give you a badge an' make you county sheriff! Now, look what he went an' done!" Cracker shook his head as if disappointed but his grin said otherwise. He lifted his cup and looked over the edge, "No other trouble?"

"Nothin' of consequence. There were some fellas that the bank clerk talked to an' I thought I might be meetin' them some'eres on the trail, an when you called out, I come close to shootin' first an' askin' questions later."

"Three of 'em was it? One of 'em a big feller, dirty lookin'?"

Cord nodded, "Ummmhmmm, you see 'em?"

"They passed about an hour 'fore you come along. Prob'ly waitin' up the trail...but that ain't the worst of the problems. After you left, a fella came into the store and was talkin' to Mike, said he saw a war party of renegade Utes led by that'n name o' Nicaagat, some call him Cap'n Jack. He said he saw them but he din't think they saw him. He understands a little their lingo and said they was talkin' 'bout some wagons with goods comin' along this here road from Denver and they was lookin' fer it. He seen them back yonder a ways, kept to the trees they did, but I seen 'em too. I think they might be layin' for them freighters that passed by earlier this mornin'."

"How long you been here?" asked Cord, frowning at his friend.

"Made camp yestiddy, figgered you do alright in

town. See you got'chu some new duds an' such," replied Cracker, grinning broadly and nodding at Cord's clean duds.

"Well, when I got me a bath, I stood my britches up in the corner, thot it was 'bout time to get some fresh uns." Cord looked at the lowering sun, back to Cracker, "You plannin' on headin' back today or waitin' till tomorrow?"

"Oh, we could make a few more miles today, might could get some o' the problems resolved 'fore we turn in."

Cord knew he was talking about the three men that had talked with the bank clerk and made good time before Cord. He guessed they would be waiting somewhere on the trail and their kind would want to be far enough away from the city that their planned strike would not be seen or heard, but still close enough to make it back before too late, allowing time to enjoy the stolen loot. He tossed out the dregs of his coffee, stood and with a glance to Cracker, "We ridin' together, or you gonna follow along to bail me outta trouble later?"

Cracker grinned, "Oh, I always to my best to stay out of trouble!" he chuckled as he also tossed out his dregs and went to his tethered horse. It was rugged country they were in and when Cord returned to the trail, Cracker motioned him on and said, "I'll be along, don'chu worry 'bout ol' Cracker," and cackled as he straddled his mount.

Cord looked about, noticing the many rocky outcrops and the hills rising a good thousand feet above the stage road on both sides. Yet the road made a bend to the south and rounded the point of the close-in butte and the valley opened up to show the meandering Turkey Creek twisting its way through a flat bottomed grassy valley. The road continued south for a couple miles, then bent to the west between two lower buttes. Cord had always been a thoughtful man and now thought about if he was a highwayman and wanted to jump a lone traveler. He would want some cover, but easy access, and if he had some companions to help with the thievery, he would want a spot where they could come from both sides and be under cover until the last moment. He grinned, remembering the road from his recent travel, and knew the road would bend to the south again around a timbered bluff and open to a wider grassy valley.

He leaned back and slipped his coach gun from the scabbard that lay across the back of the cantle and lay it across his legs and the pommel of his saddle. He always kept his guns loaded, and he chuckled as he cocked the hammers on both barrels of the shotgun. As he rounded the low bluff, he grinned as he saw tall ponderosa on both sides of the road and guessed they'd be hiding there, they would not have had enough time to go much further and pick their spot. He nudged Kwitcher to the center of the road, allowing open space on both sides. He lifted the coach gun to rest the butt on his right thigh, used his left hand to slip the loop from the hammer of his pistol, and watched as Blue dropped back, glancing to Cord and looking to the trees as he lowered his head, growled and showed his teeth. "Easy boy, I know," he nodded to the trees on his left, "I'll be countin' on you to take that'un."

Blue turned to look at Cord, back to his left and trotted in his attack stance just ahead of the grulla, still growling. They came from the trees, two from the right and one from the left, all with neckerchiefs over their faces and guns drawn. The leader was the man in front on the right. He had spurred his mount to jump from the trees and was having to focus on handling the spooked horse, but he growled, "Stop or we'll shoot!"

The man beside him was distracted by the nervous mount of the leader, and glanced to his partner, just as Cord lowered the barrels of the coach gun and pulled both triggers. The blast from the coach gun spat smoke and death, the thunder racketing across the narrow vale and the horses screaming as they took a bit of the shot from the gun. Both men were caught in the blast and their chests and bellies blossomed red as they were lifted from their seats, jerking on the reins and further frightening the horses, both dropping their heads between their legs and kicking at the clouds with their hind legs. The two riders tumbled to the ground just as Cord dropped the coach gun and grabbed his pistol from his hip, a bullet whipped past his head and he looked at the smoking barrel of an angry man that was squinting, snarling and shouting, "You kilt 'em!" just as Cord's first bullet from his pistol took the man in the throat, silencing him as he fell.

Kwitcher had held steady as did the mule, Blue went to the downed men and sniffed, ensuring they were dead. He lifted his head to Cord, smiled and let his tongue loll out as he trotted back to Cord and Kwitcher. Cord swung to the ground, went to the three men, first to the lone gunman, saw his sightless eyes staring at the clouds. Then to the two men that lay crumpled near one another. The first man was face down, one hand underneath his middle, the other stretched out as if grabbing for help. His legs were twisted, and blood stained the grass around him.

The second man lay on his back, his eyes moved to Cord as he approached. The man glared at Cord, growled, "You kilt me!"

"Well, the conversation kinda waned, and it seemed like the thing to do, 'sides, you did it to yourself when you joined up with this outfit. Did you expect to die of old age or sumpin'?"

The man let his last breath slip from his lips, and his eyes went sightless. Blue dropped to the ground beside Cord as Cord shook his head. He heard Cracker come up behind him and turned to look at the old sourdough, "They didn't give me no choice," he pleaded.

"What, did you think they'd say *please?*" chuckled Cracker. "Let's drag 'em off the road, and go find us a camp and fix sumpin' to eat, what say?"

"Don't you think we oughta bury 'em?"

"Nah, buzzards'll take care o' that, but we should strip the horses an' turn 'em loose."

32

UTE

THE LOW RUMBLE OF DISTANT GUNFIRE BROUGHT CORD AND Cracker awake as Blue rose and growled, looking to the southeast. Their camp was well obscured in the trees, but the gunfire seemed to be coming from over the slight rise south of their camp where the road bent around another bluff and out of sight. Cord came to his feet, started packing everything in the panniers and more, as Cracker pleaded, "You gonna run off and get in a gunfight without coffee?"

Cord grinned, nodded, and tightened the girth on Kwitcher, "You can stay if'n you want, but I've seen plenty of sign of a wagon train passing this way before us and a stage, could be any of them and they might need a little help. After all, I am a federal marshal now, remember?" he chuckled as he swung aboard his grulla. Cracker had mumbled as he threw his saddle on his mount and tightened the girth as Cord rode from the camp, "Wait a bit, I'm comin'!"

Cord led the way as he angled across the face of the tall butte with a rocky crown. The stage road bent back

to the west around the point of the butte and as he
neared the crest, he stepped down, binoculars in hand
and using a couple piñons as cover, scanned the
roadway and valley before him. Smoke rose from the
road beyond another bend, intermittent gunfire, and
the screams of war cries rose into the early morning
stillness. Cord scurried back to his mount, swung
aboard and with a nod to Cracker, said, "They're
beyond the next rise, c'mon!"

They dropped over the ridge, across the swale and
up the lower timber-covered ridge before them, only to
stop beside a big ponderosa to look below. A wagon
train had circled up for their night stop in a bit of a flat
with a few scattered trees, some brush, and a little
spring-fed or runoff creek. But now smoke was rising
from several of the wagons, bodies were strewn about,
and the circle was receiving fire from the trees below
Cord and a few scattered shooters on the far side of the
flat. Some of the natives were mounted and making
feints at the wagons, withdrawing and charging
another point, keeping the defenders busy moving
from one part of the circle to another. From what Cord
could see, the defenders numbers had been whittled
down and there were no more than a half-dozen men in
the circle. Cord slipped his Winchester from the scabbard, looked at Cracker, "You comin'?"

"I'm too old to try to sneak up on injuns, you go
'head, I'll hold the horses, an' use muh Sharps from
that big rock yonder," he declared as he nodded to the
rocky escarpment.

Cord slipped a box of shells from his saddlebags
and disappeared into the trees. It was easy to see where
the attackers were, having taken cover behind the trees

nearest the circle and with their horses nearby, for Indians would never leave their mounts too far away, and Cord grinned as he had the high ground. With a big fir as cover, he leaned against the trunk, took aim and dropped the hammer. The Winchester bucked and belched smoke and lead and the target, a big shirtless native, took the bullet in his side under his arm that held the rifle he was aiming, but his hammer did not fall as he winced, buckled and fell into the dirt. Cord had already started moving and searching for another target. Two men were kneeling behind some trees, close together, using the outspread branches for cover. Cord chose the one closest to him, picked his target as the side of the man's head, took a breath, squeezed the trigger, and watched as the bullet blossomed into red, smashing the man's head into the branches to fall in the needles below. The other shooter turned, just in time to take another bullet from Cord that shattered his bone hairpipe breastplate and drove him to his back, dead before he hit the ground. A thunderous roar came from the rocks above and behind him, prompting a grin from Cord for he knew the sound of the big Sharps in the hands of Cracker.

Cord moved back into the trees and began to circle around on the high ground to the north of the wagons. He noticed the scattered firing seemed to have subsided a little, but still continued. A quick glance beyond the wagons showed the mounted charges of the natives had stopped, but there was still firing coming from that direction. Cord heard some shooting below him, worked his way around and spotted two shooters. He found cover behind a sizable rock outcropping, went to one knee beside it and took careful aim on the first of the two. He drew a breath, was squeezing the trigger, when a bullet whanged off the rocks beside his head. Cord hunkered down in his collar, searching for the shooter. It was the second man further in the trees, but visible and taking aim at Cord again. Cord dropped to the ground, gaining cover in more rocks and heard another bullet whistle over his head. He crawled to the side, searched for the shooter, saw movement in the trees and lifted his rifle. The man stopped, searching for Cord, and Cord dropped the hammer on him. The bullet tore bark from the tree used by the man for cover, but tore into his chest and knocked him to the ground.

Cord looked around for the first shooter, but he had moved and Cord did not know where. Cord crawled back away from the rocks, went to the trees, just as a bullet ripped through his new shirt, but did little more than scare Cord to make him drop to the ground behind a cluster of aspen. He moved to where he could see in the direction of the shooter, saw the man running away through the trees and did not risk another shot. Cord searched the area nearby, neither saw nor heard any other attackers, and rose to work his way back to the horses.

When he walked from the trees, he saw Cracker standing, rifle in hand, looking below at the circle. He heard Cord, turned quickly and saw Cord with his hand raised and palm open to stop him from shooting and Cracker said, "Whew! I thought you was one o' them injuns!" he paused, looking at Cord, "They musta thought there was more of us, what with you movin' around and I did a little muh own self."

Cord came to his side, looked down at the wagons, and was surprised to see the attackers had overwhelmed them and were fighting face to face. He saw tomahawks raising and dropping and screams filling the valley. Cord replaced the Winchester, grabbed the Spencer, and went to a nearby rocky escarpment, bellied down, and began his own assault. He used the greater distance accuracy of the Spencer with the telescope and began picking off the attackers. Cracker had also found another rock to use for his assault and the big Sharps added his deep thunderous road to the assault.

Cord had dropped three and Cracker another two before the natives noticed what was happening. With screamed war cries, probably assuming there were more shooters than they knew, the natives went to their horses, and rode into the far trees. Cord waited, searching for other targets, but silence fell on the valley, the only sound coming from the wailing wind moving through the pines that sounded like mournful cries.

Cord went to his mount, slipped the Spencer into the scabbard, saw Cracker doing the same, and with a stoic expression, led the way from the trees to the wagons. He called out, "Hello the wagons! We're friendly and comin' in!" But there was no response and Cord reined Kwitcher to a space between the wagons that had been used by the attackers, and slowly rode into the circle. There were bodies all about, men and women, and at one wagon, a young girl and a boy of about twelve lay with sightless eyes staring at the late morning sky. A moan from the side caught Cord's attention and he turned to see a grey haired woman crawling from under a wagon, wide eyes staring at Cord and a mumbled, "Oh, thank God!"

Cord dropped to the ground and went to help the

woman from her hiding place, and as she slowly stood, and trembling to look around, her hand went to her mouth and she looked around the area nearby, "My husband, where's my Homer?"

"Ma'am," began Cord, grabbing at a chest that he pushed next to the wagon, "Why don't you be seated here and let me look around."

The woman nodded, her trembling hand at her mouth and wide-eyed she came to the chest and looked at Cord, reached out for his arm, "You'll find my Homer, won'tchu?"

Cord nodded, and helped her to be seated, turned away and began his search of the wagons, looking for any that remained among the living. Cracker had started around the circle the other way, and they were searching around, in, and under all the wagons, at least those that were not burning and there were several that still smoldered. As they made the gather, they sent the survivors to the lead wagon where Homer's wife waited. When Cord approached the last wagon, he saw a buckskin clad person, one foot on the tongue of the wagon, searching the trees behind the circle, watching for movement. Cord asked, "See anything?"

A scratchy growl came, "Nothin'. Reckon they done run off!" The buckskinner turned and Cord was surprised to see it was a woman, who frowned at Cord, "Who're you?" she asked.

"I'm Cordell Beckett, who're you?"

"I'm Blossom Boone, I scout fer this outfit. You the one what was shootin' down from the trees?"

Cord nodded, turned and pointed to the lead wagon, "We're gettin' folks together o'er yonder by that wagon. It'd be good if you'd go there so we can get goin' and git outta here, I'm thinkin' them Ute will be comin' back."

Blossom took a last glance to the trees, picked up her Henry rifle and sauntered to the lead wagon. Cord watched, shaking his head at the wonder of a woman being a scout for the wagons, and a good lookin' one at that. She was a short-haired blonde, most of the hair tucked under a floppy felt hat, and she filled out the buckskins like no one he had ever seen. She wore britches fringed at the side of the legs, moccasins, and the tunic was beaded across the upper chest and back, accenting what they covered. Cord thought she looked better in buckskins than most women look in dresses, and that included the native women. He let a grin split his face until he heard a whimper come from another wagon. He walked to the back of the nearest wagon, pushed aside the canvas and looked into wide frightened eyes of a pair of youngsters with a scowling woman behind them.

"Howdy folks, I'm Cord. How 'bout you comin' on out and going up yonder with the rest of the folks."

"Are the injuns gone?" pleaded the girl.

"For now, that's why we need to get together so we can get outta here 'fore they come back!"

That was enough motivation to get the three moving and they clambered from the wagon and made a quick walk to join the others. When Cord joined the group, he looked around at the numbers. There were three men, one with a bandage around his head where he'd taken a scalp splitting bullet, one of the others had a bandage around his upper arm, and the third only showed fear in his eyes and in his nervous movement. Four women, the older grey haired one, the mother of the two youngsters, another matronly looking woman of about forty, and Buckskin Blossom. The two youngsters were the only children. Cord guessed there were twenty to thirty bodies of the people from the wagons scattered about, and overhead, the turkey buzzards were circling.

33

RETURN

"FOLKS, NEAR AS I CAN TELL, WE GOT TWO WAGONS AND teams. We need to quickly get loaded up and get outta here 'fore those Ute come stormin' back. Chances are they been watchin' us, or at least left somebody behind to watch. They prob'ly thought there was more of us than just me'n Cracker there that was shootin' from the trees and made 'em scatter. When they get that figgered out, they'll probably come stormin' back. So we need to get gone from here fast as we can."

"But, but, aren't we gonna bury the dead?" pleaded the middle-aged woman who was known as Rowena. "My husband's lyin' over there!" she pointed with a trembling hand, holding the other to her mouth to keep from bawling.

"Ma'am, if we take time to bury them, we might hafta jump in the graves with 'em."

"But, it's not decent to leave 'em like that!"

"I don't think they'll be doin' too much complainin' ma'am, and I reckon if they could have their say, they'd probably agree with me and tell you to think of your own safety. Don't you think your husband would want you to go on living?"

The woman sobbed and sniffled, nodding her head and turning away.

Cord said, "We'll be takin' these two wagons here," nodding to the two behind him, "and if you men would get the teams hitched up, and if there's something you just hafta have," he looked at the others, "you best be gettin' it and get back here to the wagons."

He walked around, looking at the wagons and more, then added, We're fixin' to leave just as soon as we can. Now, get movin'!" motioning with a wave to the group.

The men turned to their task, talking to one another as they gathered the teams together and started putting on the harness. The women talked among themselves, nodding and pointing and the scout took control and told the others what to fetch and what to leave. Blossom then turned to the two wagons, looked inside and stepped into the back of one, started throwing out some of the unneeded things, did the same with the second wagon and soon stood beside the lead wagon with her Henry cradled in her arms before her, her saddled buckskin mare tethered to the wagon behind her, and a grim smile on her face as she waited for the others.

There were a few sobs and mumbled goodbyes from the people as the wagons pulled out of the circle and took to the road bound for South Park. Cord had learned from the men that the wagon train was made up of both freight wagons and personal wagons. The freight bound for the settlements in the gold fields, and the wagons carrying families of settlers bound for the same lands, hopeful of making their fortunes in some cases, reuniting with men gone before to do the prospecting. The woman with the youngsters was hopeful of finding her husband in Fairplay, but the other women had lost their husbands and their future was uncertain. Buckskin Blossom, as Cord took to calling her, had scouted for other wagon trains and had no specific plans, but she smiled at Cord as she came alongside to ride the rest of the way into the Park.

"So, Mr. Beckett, why are you goin' to the gold-fields?" she asked.

"I'm not *going to* the goldfields, I'm returning. I'm not a prospector, I just made a trip to Denver for the Mercantile owner/banker of Oro City and made a deposit in the bank for him. I also had to see a couple fellas there, and now I'm headin' back." He paused, looked down at her. He was a good foot taller than Blossom and her buckskin mare was just shy of fifteen hands while Kwitcher stood close to sixteen. "And what about you, Miss Boone, I assume it's miss, what's your plans?"

"Yes, it's miss. And I don't have any particular plans. I came west with my uncle and aunt. They were determined to find gold and get rich, but the natives had other plans. They were killed, I was taken captive by the Ute and lived with 'em for a couple years, learned their ways and their language, but when one o' the warriors wanted to make me his squaw, I thought it was time for me to leave. Been on my own ever since. Most white folks don't wanna be around me, think I'm too much native, and I don't have any hankerin' to be around the natives, had 'nuff o' that, so, I'm kinda alone."

"So, if you were scoutin' for the wagons, how come they got attacked?"

Blossom frowned, leaned to the side to give Cord a long look as if studying the man, "I warned 'em, they circled up and thought they oughta palaver, I told 'em not too, but some men don't think a woman knows nuthin', so..." she shrugged.

Cord understood, knowing the way of many of the whites thinking the only good Indian is a dead Indian, and others that thought you should be able to talk to anyone, including the natives, and not have to fight. But Cord knew there was no one way of dealing with any of the native tribes, each having their own ways and traditions.

"So, you were with your aunt and uncle. What about your own folks?"

"They were killed in the war. My father was a minister, and my mother did some nursing. At the battle of Lexington, the first one, my father had been a teacher at the Masonic College in Lexington, Missouri, and was killed during the battle. My mother served as a nurse, and coincidentally, was killed at the second Battle of Lexington. After that, Lexington was known as the center for Quantrill's Raiders, who you might know a little about since some o' them are still doin' their dirtywork!" she snarled, shook her head at the thought and memory, and dug heels to her buckskin to move ahead, presumably to do some scouting. Cord watched as she rode away, wondering about her and thinking of the similarities between them. They were both from Missouri, both had fathers that were ministers, both had been impacted by Quantrill's Raiders or Red Legs, and now both were alone. He smiled as he thought of her, realized he was attracted to her, and shook his head for now was no time to get tangled up with a woman. Now he had more of a job to do than before, since his appointment as a deputy U.S. Marshal.

Cord did not see Blossom again until after they pulled into Bailey's Ranch just after dusk settled over the mountains. She was sitting on the porch of the hotel, feet up on the rail, and watching as the two wagons rolled past the hotel to stop beside the corral behind the barn. She grinned and nodded as they rode past and once stopped, Cord had them unhitch, strip the horses and lead them to the creek for water before turning them into the corral. "Once we got things settled, you can fix up some supper or go to the hotel and eat at the café. But we'll be pullin' out at first light, so what'chu do is up to you." He saw the concerned expressions on the women's faces and he stepped closer to the group, lowered his voice, and asked, "You ladies are gonna be alright, there's food in the first wagon, 'nuff to go round for the next few days, but..." he paused looking at each one, "Me'n Cracker's gonna go to the restaurant, an' might even get a room at the hotel. Now, here's what I'll do for you all, any of you that want to eat with us at the restaurant, you just come ahead on, whenever you're of a mind, and me'n Cracker will be happy to have you join us and we will treat you to supper."

Elvira Munson stepped forward, "I'm too old for all that galavantin', I'll just stay here to the wagons and if'n I can get one o' the men to build me a fire, I'll cook up some supper here for whoever wants to stay to the wagons." Julius Buell, the one with the bandaged head that covered his grey hair grinned a little sheepishly, looked to Elvira, "Ma'am, if'n you'd allow, I'd be happy to build you a fire an' he'p with the supper fixin's."

Elvira smiled, nodded, "That'd be fine, Mr. Buell, that'd be fine," as she toddled off to the back of the first wagon to gather up her fixings for the supper meal.

Rowena Hewitt and Mary Hallburton looked at one another, then to Cord and Rowena spoke, "Would it be alright if we brought the children?"

"Of course," answered Cord, with a glance to Cracker who was grinning broadly. He had been spending a lot of time in the company of Rowena, the middle-aged matronly looking one. "And I'm sure the scout, Miss Boone, will also join us," added Cord, glancing to the grinning Cracker.

The other two men, William Case and Patrick Chandler, followed after Elvira and Julius Buell. Case and Chandler had kind of partnered up, both had been freighters that were looking for an excuse to try their luck in the gold fields and the attack and destruction of the wagons had provided that, and now the men were busy making plans for their future in the gold fields.

Blossom Boone was standing on the boardwalk in front of the hotel as Cord and Cracker walked to the hotel and restaurant. She greeted them with, "I thought you'd be wantin' to have a good meal and maybe even a room with a bed," she chuckled.

"Well, we invited the ladies to join us for supper and I thought you'd like to have supper with us as well, what say?" invited Cord.

Blossom nodded, and as Cord stepped up on the boardwalk she sided him and they walked into the restaurant together, both wearing broad smiles. Cracker chuckled as he followed and helped push a couple tables together to seat everyone as the women that were the servers set the table with dinnerware and cups, all filled with steaming hot coffee. Cord seated Blossom between him and Cracker, sat down to her left and as the other women and children entered, he stood and helped them be seated, then returned to his seat. He looked at the others, "The ladies here said the special was beef stew with potatoes and onions and gravy, biscuits, some greens, and...somethin' else I can't remember. But they did say there was pecan pie for dessert!" he declared, grinning at the smiles all around.

It was a pleasant change for everyone to dine in a restaurant and have a time away from the wagons and the memory of the attack that same morning. After the dinner, the ladies were very thankful, excused themselves and walked back to the wagons, escorted by Cracker. Cord and Blossom returned to the front porch/boardwalk and sat on the long bench in front of the window to enjoy the star-filled night and quietness of the evening. They sat in silence, listening to the crickets and occasional night birds or the chatter of squirrels and the distant chorus of frogs. When a lonesome coyote lifted his wail to the night, both smiled at the chorus, knowing the canine of the wild was inviting company, but his invitation went without answer.

"So, Mr. Beckett, are you going to become a prospector in the gold fields?" asked Blossom.

"No, I'm not one to be diggin' in the dirt for gold or potatoes or anything else. I've got other things to think of and get done."

"And what might be more important than riches?" grinned Blossom, looking at Cord's lined face and whiskered chops in the moonlight.

"Justice."

Blossom frowned, "Justice?"

"Mmhmm, it was some o' them Raiders or Jayhawkers or Red Legs that burnt our family farm and killed my folks. Been after 'em ever since."

"That's been a few years, the war was over what, three years ago?"

"Bout that, but it was after the war when they done it."

"Oh, well, I reckon that's different." She looked at Cord, turned away and watched the quakies quiver in the night breeze, and asked, "Have you done any good since?"

"Mmmhmm. Found a few, gave 'em their due, more to go."

"So vengeance is the name of the game?"

Cord took a deep breath and slowly shook his head, "I've argued with myself about that a time or two, it's kinda hard to differentiate 'tween the two." He pulled the slip of paper from his pocket, looked at the names, some with lines through them, others remaining. "I know there's at least four left, and they recruit others to their ways all the time, so..." he shrugged, folded the paper and put it away.

"Keepin' score, huh?" said Blossom quietly, with just a glance to Cord.

He shrugged again, did not give an answer, rose and looked at Blossom, "Me'n Cracker'll be sleepin' in the barn tonight. You?"

"I'll roll my blankets under one o' the wagons," answered Blossom and rose to walk with him.

34

TRAVEL

With an early start from Bailey's Ranch, the wagons made good time. About mid-day the second day out from Bailey's, they rounded the bend that opened up the view of the expansive South Park. Cord signaled for the wagons to stop, "Let's take a break 'fore we drop into the valley. This is a good place to stretch your legs and get somethin' to eat!" he declared, as he swung down from Kwitcher and stood beside Blossom as she leaned on her pommel gazing at the vista before her. She smiled, glanced to Cord, and said, "The last time I was here, it din't seem so big," she nodded toward with wide flats below them, "an' lookee yonder, there's some buffler this side o' that little knob."

Cord chuckled, enjoying her banter, and said, "Might as well step down, I think the ladies are fixin' some food for ever'one o'er yonder by that little cluster of aspen," as he pointed to the others gathering around a little fire that already had a coffee pot dancing.

Cord had yet to pin on the marshal badge, preferring to keep it in the pocket of his duster, nor had he told anyone other than Cracker of his now official capacity. He was also remembering just a few days back when he came on the stage hold-up and had to intervene at this same place. A quick glance over the edge of the road showed the burial site of the outlaws, although it was an unmarked grave like so many in the wilderness that were remembered only by those that were responsible for the deaths or did the burying. He grew a little melancholy as he remembered other graves, especially those of his family. There had been too many times that he was personally involved in the making of graves, both of those he knew and those he caused. But there would be more, and he had to resolve himself to what lay before him. He knew it might be a long chase to find the other men that were on his list, and there was no telling how many would be added by the recruiting efforts of the Jayhawkers, but he also thought even the name of the Jayhawkers was more than these outlaws deserved, for they were nothing but outlaws, murderers, and thieves and deserving of the most dire of consequences the law would allow and that Cord could deliver, and he was determined to complete the task, whether he called it justice of vengeance, it had to be done. For it is only as good men do right that evil can be stayed and the wicked pay their due, but if good men stand aside, evil will prevail. And it must not prevail.

"I brought this for you," came a soft voice at his elbow. Cord turned to see the smiling face of Blossom at his side. She handed him a couple biscuits that sandwiched thin slices of beef that still sizzled having been plucked from the pan by Blossom. Cord grinned, looked from her to the offering and said, "Umm, looks good.

Reckon I'm hungrier than I thought. Thank you!" he said before taking his first bite.

She smiled as she sat down on a big rock to watch Cord enjoy the food, looked to the wide vista, and asked, "So, what're you gonna do after we get these wagons to Fairplay?"

"Well, I've got a package to deliver to Mike Densmore at the Mercantile in Oro City. It's o'er the mountains from Fairplay. Then..." he shrugged, taking another bite.

"Then you goin' after the rest o' them on your list?" she asked, frowning.

"Maybe."

"Why didn't you just stay there and track 'em down?"

"They weren't doin' much, and I didn't have the authority to just jail 'em or anything, so, it was a matter of catching them in the act, and ..." he shrugged again.

"That had to be frustrating. So, if you din't have the authority then, what's different now?"

Cord chuckled, reached into his pocket and pulled out the marshal's badge, held it in his palm as he showed it to Blossom. Her eyes grew large as she looked first at the badge then at Cord, "You're a Marshal?" she asked, showing her surprise.

"Shhhh...I'm not ready for ever'body to know that. But yeah, I am. That's why I went to Denver City."

"So, now you have the authority, but don't you have to have proof or somethin'?"

"Yeah, but this'll make it easier," as he slipped the badge back in his pocket. "Cracker there," nodding toward his friend that was sitting with his new friend, Rowena, "and the owner of the Mercantile in Oro City,

Mike Densmore, wanted to make me a town marshal or county sheriff, but this," patting the badge in his pocket, "gives me a little more authority. But...it also has more responsibility, so I reckon there'll be other things to deal with, you know, other outlaws and such."

"I've never been to Oro City, is it purty o'er there?"

"In places, it's just over those mountains," answered Cord, pointing to the long line of mountains that ran from north to south along the west edge of South Park.

"Hmmm, might hafta visit," stated Blossom, letting a slow grin split her face as she looked at Cord.

Cord chuckled, "Well, you could always ride along with me'n Cracker, if'n you was of a mind to."

It took another day and a half of travel as the wagons trudged south across the park to make it to the burgeoning town of Fairplay. Dusk had lowered its curtain and the last color of the sunset hung over the shadowy mountains at its back as they rode into Fairplay. They pulled up out front of the Fairplay Hotel and unloaded. Cord, still sitting astride Kwitcher, leaned on his pommel as he looked at the small group, "The hotel there'll put you up a couple nights till you get things figgered out a little, and they've got a good restaurant there also. So, I'll be leavin' you folks come mornin', I've still got a ways to go." He looked over to Cracker who still sat on his horse but he was beside the wagon where Rowena was sitting, "You comin' with me in the mornin' or..." he said and grinned.

Cracker glanced to Rowena and back to Cord, "Oh, we'll see, come mornin'."

Cord nodded, glanced to Blossom, then told the

others, "I'll be sleepin' in the livery with the horses, so if I'm needed, you know where to find me. Otherwise, I'll be leavin' 'fore first light."

He reined around, glanced to Blossom and Cracker, and nudged Kwitcher toward the livery on the west edge of town, the mule kept pace with Kwitcher and Blue led the way. When he came to the livery, he was greeted at the big door by a tall, lean man with scraggly chin whiskers, who asked, "You needin' place for them animals?" nodding to the horse and mule.

"That's right, and if you got a loft or...I'd like to stretch out my bedroll also."

The liveryman frowned, nodded past Cord, "What 'bout her?"

Cord turned to see a smiling Blossom on her buckskin just behind the mule. She nodded and answered for herself, "Yeah, I'd like to use the loft too, if'n there's room."

And as Blossom spoke, Cracker chimed in, "Me too!"

The liveryman looked from one to the other, "Don'tch'all know what a hotel is?"

"Yeah, but our horses are better comp'ny," answered a grinning Cord.

———

THE SUN HAD YET to make its presence known when Cord led them from Fairplay. Four riders, because Rowena had succumbed to Cracker's charms, four horses, one mule, and one dog, made little noise in leaving the sleepy settlement, although a few early risers and at least one lop-eared dog did see the tails of the horses as they swished their way out of town. The trail hugged the south face of the hills that stood above the Middle Fork of the South Platte River until the valley opened wide to show the flanks and eastern slopes of the Mosquito Range that held at least a half-dozen mountain peaks that stood above thirteen thousand feet and a couple that passed fourteen thousand.

The slow-rising sun began to paint the granite tips of the mountains in shades of orange and pink well before the light ever touched the black-timbered skirts. The four riders rode silently, enjoying the solitude and the revelation of the Creator's magnificence as He slowly brought light to the lonesome valleys. They followed the Middle Fork for about four miles until the confluence with Mosquito Creek, where they turned to the south to follow the Mosquito Creek Trail to the headwaters in the high country, and stayed on the trail that would take them over Mosquito Pass.

It was a bright sunny day and the air was warm, so much so that Cord had to repeatedly look at the surroundings to make sure he was still on the right trail, but when they rode the ridge and dropped onto the switchbacks, there was no mistaking the glaciers in the crevices and cuts in the mountain, and the air had chilled considerably. But they pushed on and when the setting sun was in their face, they saw the buildings of Oro City.

Cord reined up, turned to look at Cracker, Rowena, and Blossom, and with a smile, said, "Here we are!" and waved his arm to show the grey weathered buildings, some showing signs of life, the others staring with black eyes and closed doors. But it was home, at least for now.

35

DECISIONS

T<small>HEY RODE TO THE BACK OF THE</small> M<small>ERCANTILE, SAW A LIGHT</small> within and stepped down. Cracker led the way into the rear of the mercantile, followed closely by Blossom, Rowena, and Cord with his saddlebags over his shoulder. Mike heard them come in and since it was getting dark, he wasn't sure what was happening and met them at the door to the mercantile, shotgun in hand.

Cracker chuckled, "Now that ain't no way to greet some friends!"

"Cracker! You ol' coot! Don'tchu know that's a good way to get yore britches full of buckshot?!" chuckled Mike, lowering the shotgun, grinning ear to ear. "I been wonderin' if an' when I'd be seein' you." He craned around to see the smiling faces of Blossom and Rowena and the shadowy form of Cord behind him. "Well, hello! If you're Cord, you sure have changed—and for the better I might add!"

"Why, you're just as blind as Cracker!" declared a grinning Cord, handing the saddlebags to Mike, who traded his shotgun for the bags and went to the counter.

The store was empty and Mike asked Cracker, "How 'bout'chu lockin' the front door an' turnin' 'round the sign to show I'm closed."

Cracker grinned, hobbled to the door, moaning about old bones and more as he moved. Cord looked at Mike as he dug into the saddlebags. "Oh, by the way, Mike, this here's Blossom, Blossom Boone. We picked her up 'fore we got to South Park an' she's been follerin' us ever since! And the lady there is Rowena, she's a friend of Cracker," he chuckled as he looked from Blossom to Mike, just as Blossom slapped his shoulder.

"That ain't so! These two were so lost I felt sorry for 'em and had to escort 'em home so they wouldn't get lost again!" grinned Blossom.

As Mike began withdrawing the cash and stacking it on the counter, Blossom's eyes widened and looked from the cash to Cord, "You been carryin' that all along? I ain't never seen so much money! What'chu doin' with that?"

Cord chuckled, "Oh, just swapped it out for a little gold dust that Mike asked me to take to Denver City."

Blossom looked from Cord to Mike and back, "I knew there was somethin' different 'boutchu, but..." she shrugged, shaking her head.

Mike looked to Cord and Cracker, "Did you get'chur other business taken care of? You know..." he patted his chest as he looked at Cord, not seeing a badge like he expected. Cord grinned, reached into his pocket and brought out the Deputy U.S. Marshal badge and glanced to Blossom as her eyes grew wide looking from the badge to Cord, shaking her head, mumbling, "If that don't beat all..."

"And you took your money from this?" asked Mike, nodding to the stack.

"I did, as agreed, two hundred dollars."

"Any trouble?"

"Oh, couple times. Weren't much."

Mike glanced from Cord to Cracker, who was grinning broadly, "Told'ja!"

Cord said, "Well, I don't know 'bout the rest of you, but I'm thinkin' I'd like to get to our camp, roll out my blankets and sleep for a couple days!" He looked from Cracker to Blossom. "What about you, Cracker?"

"I'd could use some sleep, that's fer shore!" answered a grinning Cracker.

Cord looked at Blossom, "And what are your plans?"

"Well, since I don't know muh way 'round'chere, I was wonderin', you got room 'nuff in yore camp for another bedroll?"

Cord glanced to Cracker who gave a slight nod, and back to Blossom as he let a slow grin split his face, "You'll hafta do your share of camp chores!"

"Sounds fair."

Cord looked to Mike, "Could you get Rowena there a room at the hotel? Oh, has there been anything happenin' that concerns those outlaws we were talkin' bout?"

"Some, but nothin' that can't wait. You get some rest, come into town when you're of a mind, and we'll talk 'bout it. In the meantime, I'll keep listenin'," answered Mike.

———

DUSK HAD BOWED OUT and the stars were lighting their lanterns as the three rode from Oro City, taking the dim trail to cross the East Fork of the Arkansas and climb the hills to their camp. There was still some hanging meat from the elk Cord had killed earlier, left behind by Cracker but not before covering it and hoisting it high in the trees, out of reach of any predators. The camp appeared undisturbed and Cracker set about making a hat-sized fire to put on some coffee and hang some strip steaks over the fire to give them some semblance of supper.

As he poured the cups of coffee, Cracker looked at Cord and asked, "So, now what, Marshal?" and chuckled at Cord's response to 'Marshal'.

"Dunno, for sure. I'm guessin' by Mike's response, there's been nothin' happenin' around here that would lead me to believe those fellas are still around. And if that's so, I need to figger where they might have gone. What do you think, Cracker? If you were them, where'd you go?"

Cracker sat down on a big rock, put his elbows on his knees as he leaned over his cup of coffee and said, "You know, I'd be thinkin' there's till some pickin's around here. To their way of thinkin' there's no law hereabouts, so they'd have free run of the area. But... other'n that, there's a lot of diggin' and such goin' on o'er the hill. Even though some o' them towns have already died, there's others springin' up all the time. Fairplay's busy, and all up an' down those draws there's new diggin's, an' up past Como an' those other places. Don't know if you noticed but there was lotta sign south of Fairplay too. So, to answer your question, just 'bout anyplace you go you'll find prospectors and where you find prospectors you'll find those that are too lazy to dig and would rather steal, and unless I miss my guess, that's where that shiny new badge comes in." He grinned at Cord, sipped his coffee and glanced to Blossom, "And if'n I was you, I'd make Blossom my deputy and take her along!"

Both Cord and Blossom acted like they'd been slapped when Cracker said that but he cackled like he had just told the biggest joke of the day. They looked at each other, Blossom dropping her eyes first and fought to keep the smile from painting her face. Cord just shook his head and grinned, thinking it would be nice to have company as he sought out the outlaws, but... Blossom?

———

CORD SAT silent and contemplative atop the escarpment that overhung the steep slope down to the East Fork of the Arkansas. The slow-rising sun was just beginning to paint the eastern sky and Cord looked down at his open Bible. The words before him were in the book of Hebrews, chapter 13 *Let your conversation be without covetousness; and be content with such things as ye have: for he hath said, I will never leave thee, nor forsake thee. So that we may boldly say, the Lord is my helper, and I will not fear what man shall do unto me.* Cord chuckled as he read those words, remembering his father saying, "conversation there means your way of life, and without covetousness means to quit wantin' everything you don't need." His father had a way of making confusing things simple and the words before him spoke loudly, especially the part about *I will not fear what man shall do unto me.*

Cord lifted his eyes heavenward and spoke aloud, "That's what I needed to hear, God. I'm countin' on you, cuz I'm not too sure about what I'm doin', this marshal'in thing is plumb new to me, but there's still those Red Legs that need to be brought to justice."

"And that's just what you'll do," came the soft voice of Blossom from behind him.

Cord grinned as he realized she had probably been there for a while and listening to all he said. He turned to look at her, thinking she was looking mighty pretty in the muted light of early morning and her smile seemed to add light to the morning. She moved closer and sat down beside him, smiling and resting her hand on his knee.

"And that stuff about you needing a deputy, well, I think Cracker was trying to play cupid and get us together, you know, as a couple. But, right now, that might not be the best. You have to be concerned about you and your safety as well as the new job of being a marshal, so, I've got other ideas."

"Oh, and what *other ideas* do you have?" asked Cord, grinning and enjoying their moment alone and together.

She smiled and said, "Rowena lost her husband, but she has a little nest egg of savings and we were talking about maybe doing a restaurant or something like that hereabouts."

Cord nodded, and started to speak when Cracker called out, "Hey you two! Coffee's ready!" They smiled, rose, and walked together to join Cracker.

As they neared, a grinning Cracker said, "I thought we'd have a bit o' breakfast, then go down an' talk to Mike at the Mercantile. He was actin' like he knew somethin' we oughta know, so..." he shrugged and started pouring the coffee.

They made short work of breakfast and before the sun was high over the mountains, they rode into Oro City and walked into the Mercantile. Mike was talking to Rowena who smiled broadly at Cracker when he entered, and a nod and a wave from Mike motioned them to the pot bellied stove in the corner. Even though it was early summer, the nights were cool and the warm stove felt good as they gathered around, each holding cups of fresh coffee and taking a chair in the circle.

Mike started with, "I've been talking to Rowena and she was tellin' me about the idea she had about a restaurant and as you know, most of the businesses in town have folded up, but..." he grinned as he paused, looking around, "there's things happenin' all the time in the gold fields and I listen. Now, here's what's new, over to Blackhawk, there's a fella that built him a water powered arrastra, that's a rock busting contraption, and another'n o'er there also built a smelter."

"But what does that do for this country?" asked Cracker, frowning.

"That's what I'm getting at, those things help miners process lode gold, you know, the kind that's in the ground, veins, an' such, and has to be broken up or blasted out, but is a lot richer than the placer gold that's been taken so far. And it's because the placer gold, the easy to get gold, has played out, that's why so many have left. But..." again he paused, grinning, "I have learned there's been a recent strike just up from here in lode gold and it promises to be a rich one. And not only that, another fella, calls himself a geologist, said he thinks all this black sand that's been clogging up sluice boxes, just might be high in silver." He grinned as he looked around, seeing the surprise and confusion on the faces of the others.

"What that means is, the gold rush we had before, ain't nuthin' compared to what's about to happen to this country! So, when Rowena talked about a restaurant, I think it's a plumb good idea! And not only that, I'm willing to help put up a hotel and restaurant, after we get the restaurant goin', that is."

Rowena was almost bouncing on her seat and reached over to take Blossom's hand, nodding and smiling. She said, "Blossom, it's just what we need. You an' me, why, we'll feed them hungry miners and more, and who knows what all can happen!"

Blossom clasped Rowena's hand, smiling and nodding. She glanced over to see Cord frowning and appearing quite thoughtful. Cord looked at Mike, "You also said you had somethin' that I needed to know."

"Ummhmmm, that's part of it. But also, I heard a couple fellas talking about a bunch that did not look like prospectors and were lookin' like trouble, and the way he described them, I know they're the ones you were after. He said they were talkin' about goin' over Weston Pass and see what they would find in South Park, but once the word gets out about this lode strike, I think they'll be back. That kind always follows the new strikes where the miners are more interested in getting the gold than they are about protecting it."

"So, since this," Cord was holding the badge in his

hand at his side and nodded to it as he looked back to Mike, "was partly your idea, what is it you think I should be doing? After all, my main purpose has been to find those Jayhawkers and bring a little justice."

"Well Cord, I reckon that's up to you. You could go back o'er to South Park, look around, or you could look around this country. We don't know if they left, didn't you say they had a camp up Porcupine Gulch? And, then again, you might want to sort of establish yourself an office here in town so folks'll know, there's law an' order come to Oro City! And I've got somethin' for you." He reached around behind him, pulled out a black book, "I understand you do a bit of reading and you have your Bible, but this is something that you'll find mighty interesting, it's Blackstone and his Commentaries. It's considered the most important book about the basics of law and it's used by judges, lawyers, and peace officers alike." He handed it to Cord, "And that will be a good start for your law library to use as a Marshal."

Cord chuckled, accepted the book, shook his head, "That's just what I was afraid of if I took this badge, I'd hafta start actin' like a real marshal!" He glanced to Blossom, saw a broad smile, and shook his head, thinking to himself, *Sometimes I just naturally fall into trouble, and other times, I just walk right into it, eyes open and all. One thing's for certain, if there's trouble, I'll find it.*

ACKNOWLEDGMENTS

As writers, we don't often get to hear from those who read our works, but occasionally, there are times that we do have the opportunity to interact with those that take time out of their busy lives to read what we have written. Sometimes, those words are chastisement, not just to criticize but to encourage us to do better. Occasionally, those are words of encouragement, even endearment, that lift us up and give us motivation to do more and to do it better. I have been fortunate to occasionally hear from readers and most often, those are words of great encouragement. And it is those words that add music to my thoughts and purpose to my work. This last year has been a challenging time for me and my wife, but invariably those words of encouragement come at just the right moment and give strength to continue. So, I say thank you, to each of you that whether worded or written or shared or just thought, form those words that keep me and others like me hard at work to provide tales and tomes for you and yours. Thank you and may the Lord richly bless each and everyone.

A LOOK AT BOOK THREE
BLACK HAWK

HONOR. RECKONING. GUNSLINGING ACTION.

Cordell Beckett carries a list of names. While several have been crossed out, six still remain. Driven by a haunting act of villainous destruction, he is on a lifelong quest for vengeance, grappling with the fine line between right and wrong. Accepting an appointment as a federal marshal, he hopes to use his position to aid his quest.

But when a wicked band of ragtags takes a young woman captive, Cordell can't help but go to her aid. Venturing into outlaw gold camps and confronting evil across the gold towns of the Rockies, Cordell faces trials that may be too great to overcome. And in a hard land where righting wrongs and bringing evil to justice demands everything, can he stay true to his mission...or will he lose himself to the darkness?

In a land where justice is bought with blood and integrity is the ultimate gamble, one cowboy must decide if vengeance is worth the cost of his soul.

AVAILABLE SEPTEMBER 2024

ABOUT THE AUTHOR

Born and raised in Colorado into a family of ranchers and cowboys, B.N. Rundell is the youngest of seven sons. Juggling bull riding, skiing, and high school, graduation was a launching pad for a hitch in the Army Paratroopers. After the army, he finished his college education in Springfield, MO, and together with his wife and growing family, entered the ministry as a Baptist preacher.

With many years as a successful pastor and educator, he retired from the ministry and followed in the footsteps of his entrepreneurial father and started a successful insurance agency, which is now in the hands of his trusted nephew. Having finally realized his lifelong dream, B.N. has turned his efforts to writing a variety of books, from children's picture books and young adult adventure books, to the historical fiction and Western genres, which are his first loves.

Printed in Dunstable, United Kingdom